Whispers of Timber Creek

S.J. Chaynie

Contents

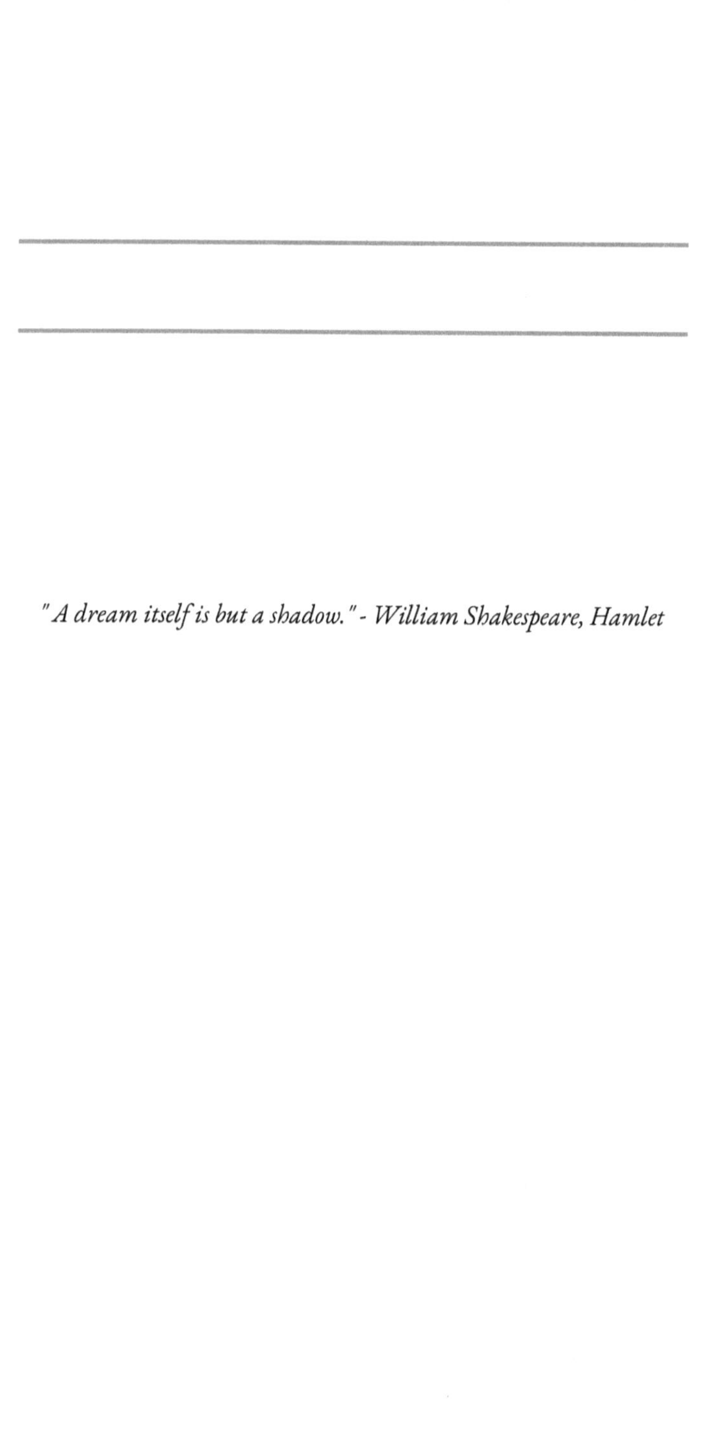

"A dream itself is but a shadow." - William Shakespeare, Hamlet

CHAPTER 1

Jace

I stare at the clock on the pale-yellow wall. This color is supposed to make you feel comfort, or so says my shrink. The woman in her late fifties who sets across the coffee table from me. She slides her red rimmed glasses up her nose for the twelfth time in the last hour. *I know because I've counted.* There is nothing else to do. Talking is something I sure as fuck ain't going to do, so I pick something out and focus on it.

"Jace, the point of these sessions is for you to talk to me." She tilts her head as she casually taps her pen on her notepad.

"I don't even need to be here. I'm fine," I answer. My knee bounces, clearly showing my aggravation to this pointless interaction.

Which I am. I'm fine. It's been almost five months. *I'm fine.*

"You know the department's stipulations. I can't let you return to field work until you've been cleared." Dr. Davis sets the notepad down on the coffee table with a heavy sigh.

"I'm aware Dr. Davis. I am also very confident in doing my job." My fingers flex as I glance at the clock again.

Three more minutes.

"I'm not questioning your skill level Detective Foster. I'm concerned about your psychological state. Your mental health." Her brown eyes drip with sincerity as she speaks to me. It almost makes me feel bad. But not bad enough.

I've been doing this bullshit once a week for three months. I spend the whole hour in silence, hoping she will get tired of my shit and give me the clearance I need. I have nothing to say. I was in the wrong place at the wrong time and got caught in the crossfire. A situation gone bad, and it was just a causality of the job. Injuries happen, and there isn't a cop around that doesn't know the chances. *Ask my partner.* Then they want to throw you on a couch while a stranger asks, "now how did that make you feel, Jace?" Like I was hit by a fucking train, Barbara. How else does getting shot in the chest feel?

"Look, I have no dreams and I'm sleeping great. I have no flashbacks and I'm still putting in time at the shooting range." I shrug. "The shots don't bother me. So, I will tell you again, I'm fine."

"This isn't just about you getting shot. It's also about your partner." She pauses. "You lost someone close to you, Jace. Those things take time to heal. Grief is different for everyone."

The timer dings, signaling my freedom, so I quickly push to my feet and grab my coat from the arm of the couch. I don't even respond to that last comment. I'm itchy all over and I just want to leave.

"I will need to see you again at the end of your three months, detective." She raises a brow as she watches me bolt for the door. "Just because we are pausing these for your relocation doesn't make them any less important or effective."

I wave a hand to let her I know heard her right before I escape into the parking lot. Hopping in my truck, I slam the door and curse under my breath. How my life could derail this much in a matter of a few months I don't have a clue. One second, I was next to my partner, zeroing in on our suspect, then the next I woke up in the hospital with multiple gunshot wounds. Then to really sweeten the pot, the news my partner, and best friend for the last ten years was dead. *Gone.* Leaving behind a wife and brand-new baby.

I pinch the bridge of my nose as I replay my last conversation with Chief Ward.

"A change of scenery would do you good, Foster," he told me as he handed me a sheet of paper. "I know you think you're ready to get back out there, but I'd rather take precautions."

"Timber Creek?" I ask as I read the black ink.

"You have three months of mandatory leave left, which means three more months off of field duty." He lifts a brow. "And that's only if I feel you don't need more time."

"I don't need time chief..."

He holds up a hand. "Jace, this is not up for discussion. I'm good friends with Captain Harper in Timber Creek, they are short staffed and he has agreed to let you finish out your three months there."

"On desk duty," I mutter.

"It takes a toll, Jace." He studies me with a sympathetic look. "Get out of the city, take it easy, and help out a small town. Get back on your feet. You've had a lot of loss in the last couple of years."

My jaw clenches. I know he's referring to Natalie.

"Look at it as a vacation. It's beautiful out there. Believe me son, it will be the best thing you ever did."

Not only is Tom Ward my chief, he was my father's best friend and partner. I know he's speaking from experience. My father was killed in the line of duty when I was seven years old. Chief has been like a second father to me since that day and has always taken it upon himself to be responsible for my well-being.

I blow out a breath as I turn the ignition. It's a long drive to Timber Creek. I'll have to make an overnight stop at some point. As I drive along the highway, I watch the scattered leaves fall. They are coated in a burnt auburn now that fall has come, and before long, when I'm in a whole new atmosphere, they will waste away to nothing beneath the layers of white snow. My thumb taps along to the quiet radio as I try to blink away the bad memories. Memories of my best friend and me drinking a few beers after a long week. Me standing next to him as he married the love of his life. My chest tightens when I think of him. The thought always crosses my mind. *It should have been me.* I haven't even spoken to Hailey since the funeral. I can't. I can't look her in the eye when I get to live and he didn't. I'm counting on chief's words. I'm hoping this *vacation* is the best thing I've ever done.

I've been at the new precinct for a little over a month now. It's a big change of pace. I went from what I thought was boring desk duty in the city, taking a hundred calls a day to my desk job here. In the Cold Case unit. You know how many cold cases there are in a town with a population of two thousand people?

Luckily, I'm done for the day. I pull up to my rent house. Well, it's four walls and a shitter. *Not the Four Seasons.* It was the only thing I could find with such short notice. I see Mrs. Stowe peeking out of her blinds as I walk up on my porch. I do the usual, give a quick nod and get in as fast as I can to avoid having to mingle with any neighbors. As soon as I push open the door and flip on the light, my first step meets ice cold water.

"What the fuck?" I mutter, lifting my boot to see water at least six inches deep across the room.

I take a few steps in, and my eyes scan to see where the leak is coming from when the pipe below my sink burst, spraying water all over my starched jeans. I stride to the bathroom, kicking in the door to see the same spray coming from under the bathroom sink.

"Shit."

I'm already soaked, so at this point I fall to my knees, maneuvering my hand around the cabinet to find the valve to cut off the water flow. I manage the bathroom, before rushing back to the kitchen to do the same.

With heavy breaths I stand in middle of the room, observing the damage. Water is past my ankles; my furniture is ruined, and I believe my cell that's in my front pocket will be needing a box of rice to survive. So much for a change of scenery.

The new scenery can fuck right off.

Chapter 2

Camille

"I guessssss, youuuuuu say..." I murmur as I dump a plate of scrambled eggs into the trash can. The Temptations, "My Girl" plays through my speaker that's propped up on my kitchen counter. I had just finished making breakfast, so I put aside at least six bagels and made a special bowl of eggs and cheese to take to Adam and Rex. This is typically my slow time. Spring and Summer is usually the busiest, then Fall. But when Winter rolls around and the holidays come, business slows a little. Which is why I'm surprised to have all four of my cabins booked for the next five weeks.

I adjust the cowl neck on my oversized sweater as I kick up the dishwasher with my foot. Dishes are in the process of cleaning and I already have clean sheets, towels, and fresh flowers in cabin one for my newest guest. The other two are already filled with two families, and the last a young couple on their honeymoon. This place is my heart and soul. I've always been a free spirit. I tend to be into nature, freedom, and good vibes. The complete opposite of my entire family. *Well, except mom.* My father is the captain of the Timber Creek Police Department and was less than thrilled at my choice to forgo college and pursue this vessel of revenue. He wanted me to become a nurse, or a teacher, or an accountant. Something more financially stable. My brother, Adam, is an officer who works right alongside him, taming the streets of Timber Creek on the daily. He couldn't be prouder that his son followed in his footsteps. My oldest sister, Whitley, is now working on her master's degree in business in the big state of California and my twin, Tilly, is making her mark. She's strong, courageous, and teaches sign language classes. She works with families who have deaf family members that need help adjusting to a healthy lifestyle. To my father's disappointment, I'm just a girl who rents out cabins and is obsessed with flowers. *Cue the violins.*

To my right, Achilles let's out a gurgled sound as he stretches, then steps out of his bed that's directly in front of the fireplace. It's his favorite spot and I knew he was ready for his breakfast.

"Here you go, boy." I bent down and placed the stack of pancakes on the floor, then gave him a good scratch behind the ear.

I had just started to wipe off the dining table when a blue Toyota truck pulled up in the driveway. I quickly swiped the towel over the wooden table and tossed it towards the sink. When the driver stepped out, I could see his gray hair blowing in the breeze through the window. He wore a pair of blue jeans with a red plaid shirt. I would guess late sixties. I watched him tug a suitcase from the bed of the truck as I stepped closer to my door, peering out the peep hole. I better show some hospitality. After all, my job relies on my ability to be an unforgettable hostess.

I quickly assessed my hair, which was quite frankly a hot mess. Thank God I was going to see Elle today.

"Stay here, Achilles. I'll be right back," I said before I stepped out onto the front porch. Achilles was a full-grown German Shepard and could be quite intimidating, but he was a lover at heart. My father bought him for me when I moved out here. He didn't like the idea of me being alone, and seeing as I had ended things with Stuart, a dog was the next logical option.

The crisp air sent a chill through my arms as I waded through the grass. I approached him with a warm smile as I crossed the yard. The man was huge. Easily around six foot five with weathered skin. Although, with the tall pines in the background it seemed to make him look small.

I stuck my hand out. "Hi, I'm Camille. You must be Mr. Sumner?"

He glanced at my hand, then shook it with a curt nod.

I pulled my hand back and tucked a random hair that got caught in the breeze behind my ear. "I hope your trip was good. The weather is beautiful today." I motion to I guess what would be consider the weather. *The freaking air.*

His eyes flicker around, as he shifts on his feet. Okay, not very vocal. Not a problem.

"I can show you to your cabin. You will be in number one. It's right past that cluster of trees." I fish the keys from my pocket and turn in that direction.

I can feel him trailing behind me. The pines crunch under his heavy boots with each step he takes. I climb the porch, then unlock the door and lead him in.

"If you need anything my number is on the notepad by the bed. I typically have breakfast available in the mornings if you are ever hungry."

He takes in the room, before placing his lone suitcase on the floor.

"Thank you, Camille," he says with a voice just as weathered as his skin.

"You are very welcome. I hope you enjoy your stay."

With that, I leave Mr. Sumner to get settled and decide to do a sweep of the property. It's a nice morning. I could use a little fresh air. I walk along the edge of the lake. The morning dew rises along the bank, spreading a foggy layer across the smooth water. It's so quiet out here. One of the many reasons I love it. If I close my eyes, I can hear the wildlife around me. The sounds of the squirrels scurrying to the next tree. The rustle of a bird's feathers while scavenging for food. And sometimes if I really listen, I can hear the antlers of the deer that are on the back side of the mountain.

Sometimes though, the silence is too much. The wind blows a certain way and it whispers to me. It makes my skin pebble every time, so I try not to stay too long. I walk past cabin two and make my way towards three. Cabin four sits the farthest from the main house. It's across the lake and has a doc leading out onto the water. This land is beautiful, a sanctuary really. It belonged to my grandfather who left it to my father when he died, but his Will was clear on who would continue the business. *Me.* I loved the land as much as he did and the memories it held. Especially this lake. Piper Lake was a reminder for me of where I came from. A place I could try to revive my soul anytime my life crumbled around me. This place made me *feel*. I felt things no one else could understand.

That's the beauty of the whispers. They're only for me.

CHAPTER 3

Jace

A shrill singing voice pierces my ears, causing me to groan in protest. Pain shoots through my lower back as I try to maneuver myself on Adam's couch. *I'm too fucking old for this.* Not that I'm complaining. After the shit show at my place yesterday I needed somewhere to crash. Luckily, I had made some friends since I've been here. Adam Harper and Rex Carson are roommates and work with me at the PD. Adam was just promoted to Sargent, and has been showing me the ropes.

I reach for my phone, digging it out of the rice box I stuck it in last night. Holding the button down, I say a prayer and send a thanks to the man upstairs when it powers on. My hand scrubs across my face and I'm drawn back to the voice sailing through the kitchen. I check the time. It's 7:45AM on a Saturday. Who is this cheery in the mornings? Adam stayed with his girlfriend last night, and Rex may be in touch with his feminine side, but even the pitch of this voice is too high to be his, so I don't know who the hell is in his kitchen.

I roll off the couch, arching my back to somehow set my spine back in place. My bare feet hit the hardwood floor and I stand, heading straight towards the annoying as fuck musical going on around the corner.

When I round the bar, I come to a halt. My hand grips the door frame as I watch a leggy blonde wearing a baggy sweater reach up into the cabinet on her tiptoes. She comes back down on her heels, never ceasing the off-key song she's wailing at the top of her lungs. Her hair is piled on top of her head with a few unruly pieces that have fallen, framing her face. I can only see her profile, but I can already tell she's beautiful. *Young, but beautiful.* I finally push off the frame and step into the kitchen.

"You should probably keep your day job," I offer.

She startles and screams, launching the bagel she was preparing straight at my uncovered chest. It hits me right between the pecs, causing cream cheese to splatter across my skin before it falls to the ground.

"Crap!" Her hands fly to her mouth. "You scared me!" Her hands fall away, revealing perfect pink lips. Her cheeks flare red and the widening of her eyes expose the ocean blue color that radiates from across the kitchen.

"You hit me with a bagel," I grumble.

"Who the hell are you?" She snatches a butter knife off the counter that's still coated in cream cheese and points it at me.

I really don't have the patience for this shit.

I glance down to my chest. She follows my line of site, pausing on the area for a second too long. She must realize it because she jerks her gaze up to mine. "I asked you a question?" She snaps.

"I think the better question is who the hell are you? You're the one breaking and entering. You know that's a second-degree felony?"

Her throats bobs as she grips the knife tighter. She scans my face, then I see a wave of understanding hit her features.

"You're Adam's friend. The cop? He told me you were going to be here and I completely forgot!" She waves the knife in the air, flinging cream cheese across the front of the stainless refrigerator.

I lean up against the door frame. "It's detective," I correct. "But yeah, and I guess he forgot to mention to me someone was stopping by this morning."

Her brows furrow as she tosses the knife in the sink. "I come by every Saturday morning and drop off breakfast." She glances at my chest again. "That's your fault you know. You shouldn't sneak up on people."

I tilt my head. "Well, you shouldn't be performing a Wynona Judd concert at seven AM. Some people enjoy sleeping."

She scoffs as she starts to maneuver items along the counter. "Not a morning person I see," she mutters. She puts away a bowl in the fridge before she scurries over to close a zip lock bag of more bagels.

I cross my arms, watching her. I'm not sure why I haven't even attempted to clean myself up yet.

"Your name?" She asks as she grabs her purse from the counter top.

I raise a brow. "Detective Foster."

"Detective Foster," she repeats as she walks towards me. "I'm Camille. I would say it's been a pleasure meeting you, but we both know that's a crock."

She steps up directly in front of me, the movement causing the smell of sugar cookies and vanilla to slither up my nostrils. A small smirk stretches across her face as she reaches out a finger, raking it across my chest to gather a glob of cream cheese.

With a challenging glance she brings it to her lips, sucking the topping right off. "I've got some bad news, detective."

Three minutes ago, I would have put her at the top of my stay-the-fuck-away-from list, now I'm trying my best not to get a boner in my buddy's kitchen over a woman that can't be more than twenty years old.

Her eyes sparkle with amusement. "There's an encore."

She brushes past me, belting out another line of a Judd's song as she goes. Her voice lingers in the quiet house as she leaves through the front door and I shake my head, heading straight to the shower.

This girl is nuts.

CHAPTER 4

Camille

I've met a few cops in my day. I grew up around them, and I have to admit the one I just encountered in my brother's kitchen might have set a record. He was tall, sculpted, and gorgeous. Deep blue eyes, a southern drawl, and a stone jaw. Of course, he clenched it in aggravation the entire time. He never even smiled, but I still struggled to keep my eyes from his chest that was coated in cream cheese I wanted to lick off. Despite his sex appeal, he was your typical arrogant asshole who looked down on me. He was probably a boring, control freak who color codes his canned goods and actual makes his bed every morning. *No thanks.*

I drove into Timber Creek. Downtown consists of a long narrow street lined with old brick buildings. The sidewalks have benches placed along the way where a few couples and a young mother sit, enjoying the beautiful morning. I park across from the courthouse, and hustle to the other side of the street. Mrs. V was coming in hot in her 98 Cadillac. She nearly took me out. It really concerns me she's still allowed to operate a motor vehicle at age ninety-six, but I don't make the rules. That would be my father.

The door chimed when I entered the hair salon. Elle waved at me as she blew out Mrs. Grant's hair. I gave a timid wave back, taking a seat in a chair and grabbing a magazine. I flipped through the pages, scanning the gardening section. I have a green thumb and I'm always looking for tips on taking care of my plants.

"See you in six weeks, Ruby." Elle sends off the blue haired woman who gives me a smile as I pass her.

Elle grabs her broom, sweeping up the locks of grey hair on the floor.

"You got a busy day?" I asked as I took a seat in her styling chair.

"Not too bad. My late appointment canceled, so you know what that means?" She grins as she fastens the cape around my neck.

"Not tonight." I reach up and remove the hair tie that was holding up my rat's nest.

"When's the last time you've been out?" She lifts a brow.

"I go out." I frown. "I go…"

"No. Adam's house doesn't count, Camille. He's your brother." She picked up her brush, pulling it through my tangles. "It's not healthy for you to stay cooped up out there all the time. You need interaction." She leans down to whisper in my ear. "You need some dick every once in a while."

I burst out a laugh. "I'm surviving just fine. You sound like Nay-na."

She rolls her eyes. "Just a trim?"

"Yes. It's awful." I scrunch my nose.

In the seat next to me, Gladys Russell keeps her head tilted as Reagan uses the edgers to trim up her pixie cut. "Hey Camille. How's your father doing?" She asks over the low buzz.

"He's good. A lot going on right now." I glance up to see Elle flicker her eyes to mine.

"Have they found any leads?" She asks.

"Not that I've heard. No new developments."

"It's been two days, right?" She lifts her head as Reagan shuts off the clippers.

"I heard she could have left town. Apparently, her and the ex-husband were having regular disputes." Reagan unsnaps Gladys' cape so she can stand.

"I'm sure when my father has any new information, they will hold a press conference." I assure them. "But yes, it's been two days. The missing person's report was just filed this morning."

You can feel the heavy presence of fear in Timber Creek. Another woman has gone missing. It's not the first, but every time it happens, it's like a wave of awareness. Something to remind us that everything in our area of the mountains might not be as wholesome as we hope it is. You never suspect danger in the faces of its residents. There could be a logical explanation to her disappearance, or maybe it's more sinister.

"Have you been.... assisting?" She asks hesitantly.

"Alright let's shampoo, then I'm using my hot rollers." Thankfully Elle steps in, guiding the conversation to something less controversial. "We're going out tonight."

I sigh, torn between the truth and denial. I know it's not healthy, and I know I need to socialize. But I've never been the party girl. Far from it. Since I was a teen everyone in this town looks at me different. *Since I became the weird girl.* But, one night every six months or so couldn't hurt.

"Ok. But you're buying," I compromise as I follow her to the shampoo bowl.

The Peak was packed. The band was ending a popular song just as we walked up to the bar. This was the only bar in Timber Creek and had been for all of my life. The restaurant was downstairs, but drinks and entertainment were held on the second floor of one of the old historical buildings downtown.

"What do you want?" Elle asked as we slid up to the bar.

Kyle, a guy we went to high school with smiled and tilted his chin in greeting as he came to take our drink orders. "Ladies, what's it going to be?"

"I'll take a margarita, no salt," she said before she glanced at me.

"Sprite."

Kyle winked. "Coming right up, Cami."

Elle gave me a look that told me I was a total buzzkill, but I preferred to stay sober.

"Stop it." I twisted to rest my elbows on the bar.

"There's Adam." She pointed across the crowd.

My brother weaved through the bodies, dragging Bekka and all her black curls behind him. Rex followed closely behind her, wearing a hot pink beanie. Behind him was my other half.

"Hey Bek's," I called out.

"Camille! You came!" She shrieked before hugging me.

"Don't act so surprised," I muttered into her hair.

She laughed as Adam slid a hand around her waist and guided her to the bar.

I watched the interaction. The love that was so evident between the two. I missed that. Not that my previous relationship was anything like theirs. It wasn't. It was toxic. It wasn't aways, but the good could never out shine the bad. It took years for me to see that the verbal abuse and manipulation wasn't *normal.* But he always had a way to lure me back in with false promises and declarations.

I'll be better. She didn't mean anything to me. I won't hurt you.

Like a broken record. But he did hurt me. Over and over again.

"If it isn't my future wife..." Rex struts up to me, a big smile on his goofy face.

"Just know I do sleep with a box fan, year around." I pointed a finger at him.

"I know, I know," he mumbles. "It's not a deal breaker." Then he plants a kiss on my cheek.

I've known Rex since kindergarten. He's probably one of the best guys to set foot this side of the mountain. There's a lot of love packed tight into that man, but it's never been there between us. He's like a brother and he knows I tend to be attracted to the assholes or the emotionally unavailable. *Speaking of....* A body in my peripheral has my gaze swinging from Rex to the mass of muscle now standing alongside Adam.

Detective Foster.

He's wearing a plain black long-sleeved shirt and dark washed jeans. A scowl on his face and a ball cap. He rests his arm on the bar and I can't help but gravitate towards him.

"Detective," I greet him.

He glances at me, then moves his eyes back to the bartender. "You again."

"It's me, again. And you're in luck." I point to the stage. "It's open mic night."

"Lucky me," he deadpans.

I laugh just as Kyle sets my sprite on the bar top. "Thanks Kyle."

I grab my drink, wrapping my lips around the straw before taking in the cold liquid. It's not open mic night, but he seemed so put off by my singing this morning I couldn't resist.

"Don't worry, detective. I'll sing one just for you," I purred before I stepped around his tall frame.

I sauntered over to where Elle, Bekka, and Tilly were huddled around a small table

"Hey Til." I smiled at my twin sister from across the table. "You didn't tell me you were coming."

She lifted her hands and began to move. *This one practically drug me out of the center.* She signs, pointing over to Bekka.

Bekka shrugs, and I laugh. Sounds about right. We're both home bodies. Tilly was born with impaired hearing. She's completely deaf in her right ear, and her left isn't much better. Thankfully, we were able to get her some high-end hearing aids which allow her to hear quite well when she's wearing them. She's a master lip reader, but she still struggles with her voice. She can speak just fine. She has this unique, raspy voice that we all love, but she hates with a passion. Only our immediate family and a few of her close friends get to hear it. Other wise, she will only sign. Especially in public.

"Who is that and why haven't I had a piece of him?" Elle leans back in her chair, not so subtly checking out Detective Foster.

"He's an ass," I say as my eyes catch on the man who just walked in the door.

"I would agree. He's one fine ass man," she quips before she slurps her margarita.

Elle can talk all she wants, and insinuate she would jump into bed with any man she deems worthy, but we all know it's just a front. She's been in love with the same man for years. It's complicated and she's done everything she can to let go, but I know she's not over it. I don't know if she ever will be.

"Look who's here," I mumble.

My ex, Stuart, leans up against the far wall with his dark eyes pinned on me.

"Do you want me to get Adam?" Bekka asks me.

Her hand lands softly on my arm and I appreciate the concern on her face. Both of them know what all I've went through with him. *Well, the parts I've told them.*

"No, I'm fine," I assure her.

I don't want him to think he has any effect on me, my emotions, or my sanity. I left that behind a long time ago and I'm not ever going back.

CHAPTER 5

Jace

I'm glad I only had three beers last night at The Peak. My old ass can't hang like I used to. My house being in shambles was the only reason I even went. I felt awkward sitting around Adam's house alone. Needless to say, I was grateful I was hangover free this morning when I arrived at the Timber Creek PD.

My desk is almost empty. Only the stack of folders to my right and a black phone that isn't ringing to my left. My hands twitch as I watch the squad room. The conversations, the drawing boards, and the aroma of shit coffee lingering in the air. My blunt finger tips tap on the desk top as I observe Captain Harper talking with Adam on the far side of the room. The office has been nonstop since eight this morning. The pressure of finding the missing woman is weighing heavy on his shoulders. He could use fresh eyes. An outsider's perspective. At least that's my pitch. I can assist here. I don't have to go out guns blazing. My mind is my best weapon anyway.

"You look like you're thinking, Foster." Rex stands on the other side of my desk, his Titanic themed mug in hand.

"What the fuck is that?" I asks as I push to my feet.

He glances at it, turning the cup so I can see Leonardo DiCaprio. "It's a classic. A timeless love story."

I lift a brow as I roll up the left sleeve of my button-down shirt.

"Fuck off. My sister got it for me," he mutters.

I slap a hand on his shoulder and chuckle. I could care less what he drinks out of, or the fact he has a zebra print shower curtain in his bathroom. Rex is a good officer and a hell of a shot.

"I'll never let go, Jack," I mock over my shoulder.

His eyes widen. "So, you have seen it!"

I ignore him, taking motivated steps towards Cap's office that Adam just left. If I'm going to be stuck in this town, I'd rather make myself useful. Those stacks of cold cases aren't going anywhere and we have a situation at hand that's more pressing.

"Foster. What can I do for you?" Cap rubs a hand across his five o'clock shadow before he lets his worn eyes settle on me.

"I want in on the missing girl," I state. "I know I'm on cold cases, and desk duty, but I can be a fresh pair of eyes."

He nods, looking past me into the squad room. "You wouldn't believe how many reporters I've got up my ass."

"Let me help, Cap. I'm ready to get back in the game." I let my hands settle in the pocket of my jeans.

He rolls his lips together before he snatches a piece of paper off of his desk. "Alright. Have Adam fill you in."

"I appreciate it." I nod as I step back.

"No bullshit, Foster!" He calls out as I round the corner.

I don't give a shit if it's in the office. I need something. Anything to fill the void. Fill the burning hole that's been slowly killing me. I need a project. A mission. Anything to keep me going.

Anything to ease the guilt.

I sat on the edge of Adam's desk as he faced the drawing board.

"What do we got?" I asked.

He glanced over his shoulder, then back at the board.

"Meredith Towns. Thirty years old. Last seen leaving her house on November tenth. She never showed up that evening to her mother's birthday dinner."

"Is she a risk? A runaway? Anything to point to a woman running from her problems?" I ask as I cross my arms.

A grown woman leaving town isn't a crime. Something that must be considered before we put sweat and tears into a hunt that could lead to a princess with a bad attitude.

"According to the mother, no. She is insistent she wouldn't miss this dinner without calling," he says, turning to face me. "We had to follow protocol before filing the missing person's report. It's been officially filed and per usual, the reporters and locals are all over us."

"Let me start with the basics," I said.

"It's very common to hike around here. She could just be without service. Maybe wanted to get off the grid," he suggests.

"Sounds plausible. I can start with her where abouts the last week or so. The locals don't know me, it may be to our advantage," I offer.

"Sounds good to me. I'm working on requesting surveillance footage from the station across from her house."

He has an odd look on his face, and then it occurs to me. "Did you know her?"

"I went to high school with her. We weren't exactly friends, but I saw her around." He shrugs. "She was a nice girl. Kind of a loner."

I didn't grow up in a small town. I may have never passed the same girl twice at my high school, so it wasn't something I could really relate to.

"I'll get started." I stood to retreat back to my desk.

Just as I passed Easton Roy, I heard a whistle.

"It's our lucky day boys." Dustin West, the douche bag of the PD leans back in his chair.

Easton turns his head and I follow suit to see what he's referring to. Camille's long, jean covered legs are carrying her across the squad room. A smile is in place and her blonde hair in a braid. She has a large basket in her hand as she waves like she's in the running for mayor.

"Just a matter of time." Dustin eyes her like a bulldog waiting for a piece of meat. "I'll put down money that says she'll be in my bed by Christmas."

For an unknown reason it pisses me off the way he's eye fucking her. And that statement makes my jaw clench. I haven't meshed with him since day one.

Easton tosses an empty coffee cup at him. "You ain't got a fucking chance. Adam and Cap will cut off your junk and feed it to you before they let you touch her."

"You wanna bet on that, Roy?" His eyes continue to track her across the room and, unfortunately, so do mine.

I watch every step until she disappears into the break room. With adrenaline pumping through my veins, I sat down and got started. This was in my blood. Something I could never get out of my system.

The job. The rush. The thrill of the chase. All I wanted were those release papers.

All I needed was my freedom.

CHAPTER 6

Camille

I place the basket of goodies on the counter. I knew the guys had been working late and my comfort food always seems to bring them into better spirits. I took out the chocolate chip cookies, the peanut butter bars, and then Hank's favorite, lemonade cupcakes.

"You sure know a way to a man's heart."

I smiled at the sound of Hank's raspy voice from years of Marlboro Red's. I laugh, just as he plucks a cupcake form the container. Hank is the oldest officer we have. He's pushing seventy, but he's not ready to give up the badge just yet.

"The chocolate chip are mine." Another familiar voice pipes in.

Easton Roy.

"Only if you take one home to June," I bargain.

"Of course, I will. She loves these just as much as I do." He grins as he takes a baggie full of my homemade masterpiece.

June is precious. A head full of brown curls and the prettiest honey eyes you've ever seen. She's three going on thirteen. A handful. Easton raises her the best he can. Her mom bolted, took off to California when June was just six months old. It's been tough, but he has plenty of helping hands.

"I'm going to need her help on my pumpkin rolls for Thanksgiving." I take out the remaining sweets form the bag, organizing them according to flavor.

"She would love that, Cami." His eyes glow and I know he appreciates how much we love his little girl.

Elle and I take her out for a girl's day often. She needs women in her life who can teach her to be strong and independent. Her mother is Elle's cousin, which that in itself is a whole different story.

"Always taking care of your old man." My dad's arm wraps around my shoulder and I smell the hint of old spice.

Chuckling, I raise up on my toes to kiss his cheek. "I figured y'all could use some positive energy."

"We sure could, sweetheart."

He gives my shoulder a squeeze before Hollis pops his head in. "You got a call, Richard."

He sees me tucked under my dad's arm and a grin spreads across his face. "Cami, please tell me there's peanut butter bars."

"Freshly made just for you." I motion to the counter.

He knocks on the door with his knuckles. "Have I told you you're my favorite niece?"

He's not really my uncle. Hollis is my dad's best friend. They've grown up together since first grade.

My dad laughs. "I'm going to pretend I didn't hear that. Whitley would be devastated."

They both left the kitchen and I took my time getting everything set up before I put on another pot of coffee. From my spot at the counter, I could see Detective Foster's back. Broad and hunched. Of course, I noticed him when I walked in. I'm sure there's not a female worldwide that wouldn't. But under all that pure bred hotness, is a difficult, I'm better- than -everyone -else persona and *that* is the reason I won't look twice. Been there done that and I tossed that T-shirt in the garbage along with my self-pity and insecurities. I'm starting a new leaf. *Not being attracted to assholes.*

I heard my father's voice, gathering everyone's attention. "If you're on the Meredith Towns case, I need to brief you in the conference room."

I filled up a mug and made my way to the large room with a long wooden table. The room filled up with officers I've known most of my life. There were different expressions on each face as I settled against the wall at the back. Hank winked and I chuckled at the cupcake crumbs caught in his grey mustache. Easton gave me a respectful nod. Adam's eyes flash empathy, and Rex grinned like a fool. Other faces showed skepticism, and Jace Foster looked utterly confused.

"Meredith's car was just found near the parking area of Piney State Park. As of now we are working on a search party to canvas the area. That most likely won't happen today, but we plan to get that organized and ready by tomorrow morning." He caught my eye before he continued. "The next couple of days are important. We all know the statistics. The mountains this time of year could be dangerous. This could be a situation where she has left willingly, but until we have solid information regarding her where abouts we treat this as if her life is in danger." He pointed up at the large map on the wall. "She could have gone on a hike, got lost, passed out, or is even seriously injured. Anything. We need to explore all scenarios."

I nibbled my lip as he continued to rattle off orders to each officer. When he was finished, he pointed to me. "My office." I pushed off of the wall. "You too, Foster," he added.

I froze and glanced over my shoulder to see Jace bristle. He brushed passed me and I caught Adam's arm before he could get out the door.

"What's his deal?" I nodded towards the moody detective's back.

"Beats me." He nudged me with is shoulder. "Go easy on him."

Easy. That really isn't my style.

Chapter 7

Jace

"Why is she here?" I asked Rex.

"Who?" He mumbles as he takes a large bite out of a glazed donut.

"Camille." I watch her disappear into the captain's office.

"What do you mean, why? She's assisting on the case."

"Assisting? That girl is a cop?" I motion in disbelief.

"No, geez." He wipes his mouth with a crumpled napkin. "She like.... can sense shit."

I eye him as he takes another bite. "Sense shit?"

"Yeah.... you know..." He waves a hand. "Like see the future stuff."

"She's a fucking medium?" I puff out a laugh. "Fitting."

"Not a medium. I don't know, why don't you just ask her. She's helped on other cases that we've solved," he says over his shoulder just as captain bellows my name across the squad room.

So, she thinks she's a psychic. Sounds about right. She's too pretty for her own good. There was bound to be something wrong with her.

"Yes sir," I answer as I step into the captain's office.

Camille sits uncomfortably with her legs crossed in the chair in front of his desk.

"Have a seat." He motions.

I sit, and wonder what the hell he could need to talk to us about in private. I don't even know this woman.

"Camille..." He sighs.

"Before you start.... just.... please. Give me a chance," she says quickly. "I know it's very controversial, but I promise I will be discrete."

"Controversial? Try unreliable," I mutter.

She glares at me and I feel him throw me a hard look.

"I will allow you to assist under one condition." He reaches for a folder across his desk. "We both know what happened last time you went off on your own and I do not want history repeated."

Camille visibly swallows and when I glance back at him, I almost see remorse for the comment.

"I understand," she said hoarsely.

"Foster, you're with Camille." He nods his head towards her.

With her?

"I don't follow." My eyes bounce between him and her long braid that's resting against her shoulder.

"I'm sure this would be better than desk duty. I want you to partner up with her. She goes nowhere alone. Consider yourself her bodyguard."

Bodyguard?

"I.... uhm. Captain, can I have a word. Alone?" I lower my voice.

He drops his arms on his armrest, like he's already sick of dealing with everyone's shit. I get that, but this is not what I signed up for.

"Camille, can you excuse us, please?" He finally asks.

"Sure." She tentatively stands and slides around the chair before she quietly closes his office door.

"So, let me get this straight. Instead of working on the case with other fellow officers, I get stuck babysitting the psychic?" I scoff.

"Watch your mouth, Foster." He straightens his shoulders and I can tell I struck a nerve.

I shake my head. "I don't mean any disrespect, to you or to Camille. I just don't believe in that sort of thing and I think it gives false hope and makes the people lose trust in us and what we do."

"And I respect your opinion." His shoulders slightly relax as his gaze catches on a picture frame on the corner of his desk. "She needs this, Jace. And I need to make sure nothing happens to her. She's different. She has something.... quite frankly, that scares the shit out of me because I've never understood it."

"I'm sorry, captain. I just don't fall for that psychological bullshit."

He leaned his elbows down on the desk. "Here's the deal, Jace. You do what I tell you to and I just might be convinced to push your papers through. That's why you're here, right?"

It's the only reason I'm here. "Yes sir."

"Good. I'm glad we have an understanding," he barked as he stood form his chair.

My gut tells me this is a bad move, but I stand and call out a "yes sir" because that's what I'm trained to do. Follow orders.

"Now listen. Camille lacks discipline and control. She doesn't have the natural instinct like we do. She can be impulsive."

I'm not really sure why he knows so much about her. This whole thing seems a bit over the top, maybe even a little bias. I walk to the door, placing my hand on the stainless-steel lever.

"One more thing." He calls out. "I have one rule. This goes for every man in this office. Keep your hands to yourself." He bends at the waist, reaching for his pen and starts to scribble on a piece of paper. "Your release depends on it."

I chuckle. "What's so special about this one, Cap?"

He lifts his head and narrows his eyes on me. "She's my daughter."

Chapter 8

Camille

Jace stalks out of my father's office looking like someone just took a lengthy piss in his Cheerios. I'm sitting on the edge of Rex's desk.

"I told him," he says.

"Told him what?" I asked.

He typed something on his computer before he glanced up at me. "You know......about the thing you do. The sixth sense thing."

I flinched a little. Not that it's a major secret, but I knew how a man like him would react. "And what did Mr. Stick up his ass have to say?"

Rex cleared his throat just in time for me to see the shadow of said man, standing less than a foot away from me.

"Camille." His voice was even. "I need to speak with you."

I can already tell this is gonna be a blast.

He walked off, his body radiating frustration with each step as he headed towards the kitchen. I reluctantly sat down my coffee cup and followed. His back was to me, but the stiffness in his shoulders was visible.

"Detective?" I questioned.

I could see every muscle through the white button up he wore. They flexed as his hands lifted to brace on his hips.

I sighed. Why is he being so dramatic?

"Is there a problem?"

He turned to face me and ran a hand over his stubble. "Nope. Let's just do what we need to do to find this woman so I can get the hell out of this town."

The look on his face said more than that. He didn't just want away from this town. He wanted away from me. I just wasn't sure why.

"Then we better get to work. I'd hate to inconvenience you when there's a woman's life on the line." I sneered before I grabbed my purse. "I'm hungry. You can drive," I called out over my shoulder.

Ten minutes later we were seated at a corner table that overlooked the sidewalk downtown. This was my favorite diner and I had a mean craving for some bacon.

We ordered, then I brushed my braid over my shoulder before making eye contact with him. "Where do we start?"

"We can start with what you are even doing here?" He sat back in his chair, a cocky smirk on his face.

God, I wanted to slap it right off. He's already judging me. Just like everyone else in this town.

"I'm here to help. Just like you are."

He laughed. Deep and raspy. It made my insides tingle and I already decided I hated it. "I'm here because your daddy thinks you need a babysitter."

I had to bite the inside of my cheek to keep from spewing out exactly what I thought about him. My pastor sat only two tables over and I was already on thin ice with the church as it was. I felt his unmerciful gaze on me when we sat down. So, I kept my mouth clamped and forced out something less derogatory.

"I don't need you, detective," I gritted out.

"Camille Harper!" A sweet voice exclaimed from across the room.

Sonya Welch, who probably hadn't said two words to me since graduation, came bouncing across the room. Her welcome was not geared towards me. I knew better. She was only approaching for the man across from me. Sonya was gorgeous. She was everything I wasn't growing up and clearly, she's still holding that title.

"Who do we have here?" She crosses her arms, purposely pushing up her breasts that are already one wrong move away from displaying a nipple.

Jace faced her and I waited for his eyes to dip lower than her chin. But they didn't. *Why was I relieved?*

"I'm Sonya. Camille and I are old friend." She held out a manicured hand to Jace, waiting for him to accept it.

It took everything I had not to roll my eyes. She was never my friend in any form or fashion.

"Jace Foster." He nodded, reaching out to shake her hand. "Nice to meet you ma'am."

Ma'am? Jace Foster? All I got was "detective" and a Simon Cowell evaluation.

Sonya blushed, bringing her fingers up to fiddle with her earring. "Oh, a southern gentleman." She giggled. "I hear you're going to be staying in town for a few months."

"Word travels fast around here," Jace says as he glances at me, then turns his body back to the table.

"Well, if you ever need anyone to show you the sights, I'm free." She literally popped the cap of a pen that appeared magically out of nowhere and bent down to write her phone number on his napkin.

"There you go." She winked. "See you around." She paused, giving me a victorious look over her shoulder. "Good to see you, Camille."

I watched her saunter away before I faced Jace who was looking at his phone.

"Some things never change," I mumbled. "So, are you gonna go meet her for a quickie or can we actually get to work?"

He sat down his phone. "First of all, I'm not taking her number. I can tell by that brief conversation she's not my type."

"And what's your type? I figured men like you just needed someone willing?"

He chuckled. "My type is uncomplicated. Unattached and typically only once. I don't do girlfriends and I damn sure don't do a quickie." His gaze was back on me again. "I'm not a fucking teenage boy."

I'm glad he told me all of that. Just more reason for me to hate him. He's a womanizing man whore. *Got it.*

"As I was saying." I cleared my throat. "I don't need you, Detective Foster. This is just my father being over protective."

His arm draped across the empty chair next to him. "Apparently you do. So, you can bet your sweet ass I will do whatever it takes to convince Captain Harper to give me what I need." He sat forward, his blue eyes zoning in on mine. "If I have to follow his princess, who thinks she's got some super power around town while she plays Nancy Drew, I guess that's what I'm doing." He tilted his head. "The only thing I'm focused on is finding this woman and getting back home."

I leaned forward, just an inch, but the space between us seemed to shrink tenfold. "Then we have something in common. I want to find her just as much as you. And as for you going back home when this is all done." I leaned back, crossing my arms. "I'll be glad to help you pack."

His lip twitched, but he said nothing as our waitress sat our plates down in front of us. I'm glad we got that out of the way.

Now we can actually do something productive.

CHAPTER 9

Jace

Camille ate the last bite of her scrambled eggs then cleaned the corner of her lips with a napkin. We hadn't spoken since the food was brought out.

"So, you think she's lost in the mountain?" I asked.

She stacked all of her utensils on the empty plate. "No."

"Care to elaborate?" I said before I took a drink of my orange juice.

"Depends. Are you going to disregard everything I say because it's not in line with what you're taught as an officer?"

"Camille." There was a warning in my tone. I didn't have time for games or meaningless conversation.

"I'll shoot you straight then, detective." She folded her hands on the table. "I think we have a serial killer in Timber Creek who's taking women at the State Parks."

"That's a bold accusation," I admitted. And because I'm an ass I added, "you see that in your crystal ball?"

"Fuck you," she scoffed. "I knew this was a bad idea," she hissed as she angrily dug around in her purse.

With a quick flick of her wrist, she threw out some cash, but I caught her wrist when she went to stand. The last thing I wanted was to piss her off enough she reported it back to her father, which would send my release papers flying out the window.

I sighed. "Camille, wait."

I glanced around the diner to see all eyes on us. It was almost as if all noise ceased the second she stood. Her eyes were locked on my hand circling her wrist and my brain unintentionally noted how soft her skin was. "Please, sit down."

She slowly lowered back down to her chair and the chatter picked back up around the restaurant.

"I'm sorry...I just..." my hands swiped down my face. "You have to understand how it appears from my stand point."

"You think you're the only one in this place who thinks I'm insane? You think I haven't dealt with the whispers and accusations?" She shook her head as she peered out the window. "You really think I asked for this? That I woke up one day and was like, 'I would love to be able to have dreams of women being tortured and traumatized. It would be even better if they were real victims in my hometown, and what would really be the cherry on top is if I could feel every single fear and emotion they felt in the most terrifying moments of their life.'" She moved her eyes to mine and something unfamiliar flickered in my chest when I saw the tears well up. "You will never understand and you will probably never believe me, but you better believe that I have good intentions and all I want is for these women to be found and saved."

We sat staring at each other. It was a face off of sorts. Like this moment was when we accepted our differences and decided to work together or we called it quits. I had mixed feelings. I wanted away from her. I didn't want to be with her every waking minute, because even with the few interactions I've had with her I've had a hard time removing her from my mind and it's been pissing me the fuck off. But I also wanted her safe. I don't know why I cared. I didn't have any business caring. She was just a girl from a temporary town. One that was untouchable and one I had to keep at an arm's length if I wanted out of this with my dignity intact.

So, I swallowed my pride for the time being. "I was out of line. It won't happen again."

She nodded. "Thank you."

I gathered her cash from the table. "Give me your hand."

She lifted a brow. "You gonna read my palm, detective? I thought you didn't believe in that sort of thing."

She had a mouth on her. Quick witted *and* pretty. *A dangerous combination.* I chuckled as she placed her palm face up on the table. I laid the folded cash in her hand. I may be an asshole, but I was raised by a man that would have my head if I let a woman pay for my meal.

"It's on me." I pulled out my wallet as she eyed me before stuffing the bills back into her purse.

I stood to my feet. "Let's get back to the office." Then I motioned my hand for her to lead the way.

The afternoon went by quick. We spent most of the time prepping the plans for the search party and after, I spent another night on Adam's couch. I was grateful, but he just informed me Bekka was moving into his place this weekend. In other words, I was being evicted from the sofa. I slept like shit anyway. Not because of the sleeping arrangement, but because of what I dreamed of. *Blue eyes and that damn braid.*

I was already in a mood, so when Camille came in this morning sporting tight black leggings and hoodie that didn't cover any part of her lower half, I was even more aggravated than normal. But it was work. Plain and simple. I just had to focus on the job. Captain had just briefed everyone on the search party that would set out at 9:00 am, so the office was busy with preparations to head out to the mountain. You were never sure what you would find on a search. It could be good or bad. A successful rescue, or a devastating loss. It was a heavy day, but I know most of the residents, especially the parents, were in hope of answers.

"You ready partner?" Camille's voice came from behind me and I spun around to see her hold out a coffee cup. A peace offering I'm assuming. She smiled and it momentarily made me forget whose daughter she was, but then that one word settled in. *Partner.* The word makes me clench my pocketed hands. I don't have a partner. My partner is dead. Dead because of me.

I took the cup, and snatched my coat from my desk. "Ready when you are."

Chapter 10

Camille

The morning air was cold. I had a wool scarf wrapped around my neck, along with my headband and gloves as we were given the signal to tackle our area of the mountain. Half of the town had shown up to help search for Meredith. It's not the first time a resident has lost their life, or been consumed by these mountains. We've had hikers go missing for three days and were found safe. But I knew better. I knew this wasn't a hiking trip gone wrong. A sprained ankle, or something as simple as misdirection.

This was him.

I saw it. Just like the last three. I knew it in my bones. I knew it by the way they whispered my name. In the way they pleaded.

"Jace, you and Camille take the west side," Adam instructed, then turned to face Easton. "Easton you and Elle take the east side and me and Bekka will take the back side."

Elle gave me an unimpressed look. I nudged her shoulder with a half-smile. "You'll be fine."

She rolled her eyes just as Tilly rushed up.

Adam's face hardened. "What are you doing here?"

I'm here to help search. Her hands moved quick, then she tightened her coat around her body.

"No. We already have enough help and it's not safe," he said sternly.

She clenched her teeth and her hands went up again. *It's not safe for anyone, Adam.*

"You're different Til." He turned to face her. "If you get separated or lost... you can't call for help."

I knew Tilly like I knew my own self. She was getting angry, and an angry Tilana Harper was the last thing any of us wanted to intercept. Adam always meant well. He was our big brother. Our protector, and he was *very* protective of Tilly. There have been a few incidents over the years where she was injured and we've all had to take her condition more seriously.

I resent that. I have a voice, Adam. She signed angrily. *I'm going!*

He sighed and Bekka gently touched his arm, giving him the look that said *pick your battles.* Bekka was Tilly's best friend, so she was always on her side.

"Fine. Come with me and Bekka," he finally agreed.

Tilly beamed and Bekka winked as she followed them out of the parking lot.

My boots were secure and my eyes sharp. I was ready. I was ready to feel. I was ready for Meredith to show me.

"You ready Scrooge?" I asked Jace.

"Do I have a choice?" He said as I shoved my cell in my coat pocket.

We started along the path that led around the base of the mountain. Others were shouting her name and spreading out amongst the trees. I was on a mission. I would know the spot when I saw it. It was still vivid in my mind.

"I think we need to slow down," Jace called from behind me.

I glanced back as he stepped over a broken tree branch. "Or you could just keep up." I smirked.

He shook his head and I'm almost certain I heard a few choice words said under his breath. I slowed my pace to let him catch up to fall in step beside me.

"That had to be your sister back there."

I laughed. "My twin actually."

"I mean, y'all favor, but it was the attitude that sold me."

I laughed. "Tilly's a firecracker."

He was quiet for a moment. "Was she born with..."

"Yes." I finished for him. "Since the womb."

He nodded. "That's tough."

"*She's* tough," I said before I stopped and evaluated our surroundings.

"What's going on in that head of yours?" He asked.

I kept my eyes on the path up ahead. "I'm looking for a certain spot." He side eyed me. I could tell he still wasn't buying anything I said. I rolled my eyes. "I saw it in my dream. It's a narrow stream that runs next to a small waterfall."

He nodded. "And what is at this spot?"

I let out a deep breath. "I'm not exactly sure." The path took a right turn, but something urged me to keep going straight. "All I know is it's red."

"Well, that narrows it down," he mumbles.

"You got anything better to go off of, detective? If so, enlighten me."

He grumbled to himself, but he didn't respond directly.

We had a been searching for a little over an hour when the terrain began to get rocky. The boulders grew in size the closer we got to the edge. We reached an area where we needed to climb. I could hear the faint sound of trickling water just over the top and I was determined it was the valley I was looking for.

"Let me go first." Jace stepped in front of me, and launched himself up onto the jagged edge of the rock.

He climbed up high enough, then reached a hand down towards me. "Give me your hand."

He sure was bossy.

I gripped his hand in mine, and maneuvered my boot to the smaller rock just at knee level to push myself up. He lifted me and I swung my leg over when I got to the top. It was a steep drop down, but I could see the stream from this spot.

"There!" I pointed. "That's it."

"That's what?" He squatted, accessing the safest way down.

"The stream." I sat down on my but and inched closer as he stepped down onto the next open landing.

A few more steps and he was safely on the ground. I had one more to go. "Be careful. That last rock is slick," he warned as he reached out, offering me his palm.

"I got it." I waved him off.

Just as my boot hit the surface of the rock, I pushed forward, and I slipped. I lost my balance, and I would have landed flat on my face, but instead I landed against a hard chest. The breath flew from my lungs as my front collided with his and his quick hands caught me by my waist. But it wasn't the scare from the fall that had my stomach in a mess of flutters. It was Jace's bare hands that slid up under my coat, under my hoodie, and onto my exposed skin. My cheek accidentally grazed his as I leaned back to meet his eyes. I opened my mouth to apologize, but nothing came out. I literally couldn't form words when he still didn't move a muscle. His eyes stayed glued to mine, and he gave my waist a light squeeze. It was probably just a subconscious reaction. It was subtle, but enough to have goose bumps break out over my skin, causing an involuntary shiver to race down my spine.

"Cold?" He asked hoarsely.

"No," I whispered.

I whispered like someone might hear. Like someone might hear the thoughts in my head and know that I didn't actually hate the feel of his hands. *On me.* With that revelation, I blinked and took an abrupt step back. He cleared his throat and yanked his away hands from me.

"I'm sorry," I rushed out.

"I told you to be careful," he barked as he straightened his coat.

"And I said I was sorry," I snapped back as I adjusted my hoodie in place.

I glanced off in embarrassment and that's when I saw it. My fingers froze. "Jace...."

He stood a few feet away from me, staring off into the woods. "Next time, watch when I tel...."

I rushed over and took a hold of his bicep, turning him around. "Look."

There it sat. Just beyond where we landed, at the edge of the stream was a red scarf.

Meredith's red scarf.

CHAPTER 11

Jace

It took almost two hours for us to get someone over to collect the scarf. We didn't have anything with us for proper protocol and honestly, I wasn't expecting to find anything. Especially not the "red" object Camille had mentioned. I dulled it down to coincidence. There were several pictures of Meredith floating around. She could have been wearing it, or it could have been mentioned in conversation. I was nowhere near convinced to jump on the Camille crazy train. I was a detective. I did my job by looking at facts. Evidence. Something that can be proven in a court of law. I didn't put all my eggs in one basket on a fucking whim.

It was late afternoon by the time we made it back to the station. Everyone was exhausted and the only thing we found today was the scarf. No other signs she was even on the mountain at all. Her mother verified it was hers, so an air crew was going to search tomorrow. They were hoping to try to check the ground we couldn't cover.

I had just sat down in my chair when Cap came over to my desk. "I heard about your living situation."

I rubbed my tired eyes with my fingertips. "Yeah…it's a little unsure at the moment."

All the chaos had pushed my worry about being homeless on the back burner.

"I saw Dodge at the search today. He said it would be at least three weeks before the damage is fixed."

Dodge was my landlord. A pretty cool retired marine who did me a favor. I hadn't talked to him about the timeline of repairs yet.

"Fantastic," I muttered.

"Thanksgiving is in a week, you know there won't be any rooms available," he pointed out.

Yes captain. I know I'm royally fucked. Thank you for pointing that out.

"Good thing I got you covered," he said as he whistled at Camille and waved her over.

Her eyes met mine as she cautiously approached.

"Any of your cabins open?" He asked.

She shook her head. "No, I'm booked through Christmas."

"Hmmm." He grunted. "You still have that extra room, right?"

She gave him a confused look, then flickered her eyes to mine. "What is this about dad?"

"Jace needs a place to stay while the rental is being fixed. With the holidays, all the rooms in town are booked."

He wants me to…. oh, hell no.

"Cap that's ok. I'll manage to fin...." I started just as Camille began at the same time with, "Yeah, I don't think so."

He lifted a brow. "Camille, I've never known you to turn away anyone who needed a roof over their head."

Her lips thinned and I didn't miss how her tiny hands clenched into fists at her sides.

"Besides, I think I would be much more comfortable with Jace there knowing you aren't out doing anything irresponsible involving this case." His tone changed and so did his expression.

He did the same thing in his office yesterday and she immediately softened. His words were meant to strike a response, maybe even some guilt, and he apparently hit the nail on the head.

She took a deep breath and looked past her father, over to where I sat at my desk. "I have a room. If you want it, it's yours."

It wasn't exactly a warm invitation, but the hard stare Captain Harper was giving me wasn't something I was willing to test. He held my future in his hands and his eyes told me to comply or else.

"I'll take it." I nodded.

Cap nodded as well, then marched to his office.

Camille cleared her throat. "I'll get it ready. Come out anytime." Then she turned on her heels and left.

This was a bad idea. One that could be detrimental. I could already sense it, because if I ever found myself in a position where my hands where on Camille Harper's skin again......I know without a doubt I'd flush my career straight down the fucking toilet.

CHAPTER 12

Camille

"This is a bunch of bullshit," I state as I wrestle the fitted sheet I'm currently trying to shove over this full-size bed.

I'd like to throat punch whoever thought these were a necessity to everyday bedding.

Adam sighs heavily next to me. "Give me one side."

I do, with a little more aggression than I intended. Adam and I have always been close. He's like a second dad. When dad was an officer and worked long shifts, Adam was the oldest, so he was in charge. When mom died, Whitley attempted to step up and take on the role of caretaker, so we're a very tight nit group of siblings.

"It's not a bad idea. He needs a place to stay and dad needs peace of mind." He walks around the bed, helping me fit the sheet on the mattress.

I ignored the comment and continued making up the guest room in my house for Detective Foster. It's impossible for me to set aside the hospitality gene, so here I am, preparing as I would for a paying guest. Fresh sheets, clean linens, and of course, a fresh bouquet of flowers. He probably won't appreciate them, but I do it for all of my guest. I take pride in this place and even though I'm in no way looking forward to sharing a space with detective dick, I can't let my house be unwelcoming. It's not in my nature.

"I have a gun. I know how to protect myself, Adam. I'm not helpless, contrary to what dad thinks. I'm not stupid. Did I make a dumb decision? Yes, but I shouldn't have it held over my head constantly," I point out as I snatched up the top sheet I had folded on the dresser.

He shifts on his boots as he glances out the window. "Do you think it could have been Stuart that night? Y'all had just split up...."

"No. He's the master of manipulation, but he isn't dangerous." I fling the sheet up before smoothing it across the bed with my palm.

"Still...it's a possibility."

I shrugged silently. I didn't want to talk about Stuart. I hated unlocking those memories. I placed the comforter across the bed and stepped back to make sure everything was picture perfect. Once I was satisfied, we headed back downstairs.

"Foster should be out this evening," he called out from my porch before he closed the door.

"Can't wait," I mused sarcastically.

At 7:00 sharp I pulled the delicious roast I had prepared out of the oven. The carrots were cooked to perfection along with the mouth-watering potatoes. I had planned to drop off a plate to Mr. Sumner before Detective Foster arrived. I didn't know if he had any groceries, and I thought this was a kind gesture to thank him for choosing Piper Lake. I had already brought some cookies to cabins two and three who had a rowdy group of littles and made a chocolate cake for the couple in cabin four. I placed the meal in a Tupperware and walked along the trail up to cabin one. The sun was already down, but it was a full moon and it lit up the entire lake.

I knocked, then waited. When he opened the door, he had the same expression as the day we met. I can't really decipher it. All I know is it makes my heart ache. He looks...*sad.*

"I thought you might be hungry. I made roast." I smiled and held out the container.

His eyes moved down to it, before he nodded, then slowly reached out to take it from my hand. "Thanks."

"You're welcome. I will also have breakfast ready by 8:00 if you want to come to the main house." I was trying to be polite, but not too pushy. He seemed ready to flee at any moment.

"I'm going into town in the morning, but thanks," he grumbled before shutting the door.

I stepped off the porch, tugging my cardigan around me as I made my way back to the house. Just before I reached the porch, a pick-up truck rolled into the drive. I guess my next disgruntled guest has arrived.

Jace parked next to my jeep, then stepped out to grab his suitcase.

"Welcome to my humble abode," I greeted as he started for the porch.

He silently raised a dark brow and waited for me to get the door first.

Man, tough crowd tonight.

I pushed open the wooden door and led him through the living area. "Your room is the second one to the left at the top of the stairs. You can drop your suitcase there. I have supper ready."

He didn't respond, just tromped up the staircase to his temporary room. I pulled out two plates, piling them up before I set the table. Five minutes later, he came down to join me. Achilles growled from his spot by the fireplace and I couldn't hold back the smirk that graced my lips. He took the seat across from me and I cleared my throat when he picked up his fork.

"Do you mind if I say Grace?" I asked.

He paused, then glanced up at me. "Not at all."

We bowed our heads and I said a quick thank you before we dug in.

He ate, but didn't speak. The awkward silence stretched between us and since I was never good at avoiding small talk, I blurted out the first question that popped into my mind.

"So...how much damage was done to your stuff?"

He swallowed his fork full of potatoes. "Furniture is ruined. Luckily my clothes weren't."

"Before...back home, where did you live?"

He leaned his corded forearms on my table and it took everything in me not to gawk at them. He clearly works out and it just occurred to me that arms may be what does it for me. *Seriously, Camille? Arms?*

"Are we really gonna do this? Play twenty questions?" He forked an orange carrot. "I'm not really in the mood."

I scoff. "I'm trying to be civil. You're living in my house now for God's sake."

"Yeah.... thanks to your daddy."

"I can assure you I'm just as displeased with this situation as you are." I tossed down my napkin as anger swelled inside me.

What an asshole. He hasn't even thanked me for dinner, not that I need the praise or anything. It's just good manners. I was under the impression they taught that in the south.

"Just leave your plate when you're done. I'll clean it up." I stood, then headed for the back porch with Achilles on my heels.

I was right. This is bullshit.

CHAPTER 13

Jace

I sighed as I leaned back in my chair. I was being a dick. She's more put out than I am. I'm the one invading her space and then because just like I suspected from day one, she made me fucking dinner. Like we're old pals who sit down and talk about our day. That's what my therapy sessions are for. I damn sure don't need another one. Talking is not my forte. At least that's what my ex, Natalie said. I didn't communicate and all I did was work. She wasn't wrong, but she knew what she was getting into when she met me, and she knew what she was saying yes to when I proposed. So why she decided to leave me standing at the altar on our wedding day is beyond me. She made excuses, which all seemed to be my fault. The longer it's been, the more I realize it was probably for the best. If I'm being honest with myself, I just felt like that was the next logical step. Marriage. But it doesn't mean it didn't fucking hurt. Now I just avoid relationships. It's easier. No chance of disappointment.

I finished my dinner, then scooted the chair back. I wandered in the direction Camille went and found her on the back porch, curled up in a wicker patio chair by a fire. I'm impressed she even knew how to start one.

"Look Camille..." I ran a hand down my face. "Thank you for cooking. It was damn good, but you don't have to do that for me. I'm only here because of your father...I'm basically working. I'm not here to be...."

"My friend?" She lets out a laugh. "I was raised around the police force, detective. I know how serious you take the job." She curled her bare feet up underneath her. "I don't have to be your friend. To be blunt, I don't want to be. I'm your host. I take care of anyone who stays on my property. Don't think you're something special."

I could feel the corner of my lip tilt up. It wasn't a full smile. I didn't do much of that these days. "Good to know we're on the same page."

"If you need anything let me know. I'm just across the hall," she said as she warmed her hands by the fire.

I nodded as I backed up toward the door. "Night."

Her blue eyes lifted to mine. The flames of the fire made them appear to have flecks of gold around her iris. "Night."

The sun was just barely above the mountain the next morning when I woke up. Despite the fog on the glass that indicated the weather was changing, it was warm inside the small room. I laid on my back, staring up at the knotted circles of the cedar. I was debating just going back to sleep, but that's when I heard it. *God, if you're punishing me......* Singing. If you could even categorize it as that. Camille, once again, sounded like she was a blooper audition for American Idol. I rolled over, causing the white sheet to slide off my naked body as I checked my phone.

"You gotta be kidding me," I groaned as I flipped to my back.

6:12AM. I pulled the sides of my pillow up over my ears. No use. I was wide awake now and needed to piss, so I rolled out of bed before slipping into some grey sweats and a TCPD t-shirt.

I padded downstairs and sure enough, little miss sunshine herself was flipping pancakes, wearing plaid pajama pants. *Sunshine.* I step over a full laundry basket at the foot of the stairs, then slowly walk across the room. She still hadn't noticed my presence as she mouthed the words to whatever pop song was playing. She turned her back to me and placed the egg carton into the fridge.

When she spun around, I crossed my arms. "Morning Sunshine."

She narrowed her eyes at me, but then they quickly scanned down to my sweats then back up to my face. "Good morning, detective. Hungry?"

"Sure." I settled on the wooden bar stool. "I get the impression you like to cook?"

She smiles. "I love to cook. My grandmother taught me."

I nod and lean back, accessing the spread on the granite counter top. Eggs, pancakes, bacon, sausage, and something that resembles a small muffin.

She scoops up some of each and fills me a plate before sliding it across to me. "Orange juice or coffee?"

"Coffee. No sugar."

She nods and bobs her head to the music that is still flowing from a speaker set up by the microwave. "So." She sets a steamy mug down in front of me. "It's a small town, word spreads. I don't need all the details, but I would like to know who I'm sharing my home with. I'm aware you are here temporarily as a result of being off of field duty." She leaned back against the counter and brought one leg up, resting her foot at her knee like a flamingo.

Fair enough. I would want to know the same if someone were staying in my space. I dropped the fork that was loaded down with a sausage link and reached for the hem of my shirt. I tugged it up, revealing the scar under my rib cage and the healed bullet wound on my shoulder.

She gulped as she took in my bare chest. Her brows furrowed and I dropped my shirt.

"Shooting. It's part of it." I shrugged and went back to my breakfast.

"Sorry to hear that." She gazed off to her left, like she was lost in thought. After a couple of moments, she spoke again. "I was eight the first time my dad was shot." She glanced back at me. "In the thigh. I cried for weeks because I though his leg was going to fall off." She smiled and shook her head. "He let me doctor him for a month even after he was cleared back for duty. I just wanted to be sure he was healed, you know?"

"So, you've always been this way?" I mouthed through a bite of pancake. "Over dramatic?"

She laughed. "I guess so." She snapped her mouth shut, then quickly stepped away from the cabinets. "I'll let you finish up."

She hurried out of the kitchen and up the stairs. Everything about this woman screamed at me to stay away, but the one small voice in my head was whispering something different. Something I couldn't quite understand and I wasn't sure I even wanted to.

Chapter 14

Camille

After Jace left to grab a few more things from his house, I went for a walk. Achilles needed his exercise and I needed to think. Mainly how I was going to survive three weeks with the man who took over my guest room. After a good hour, I circled back to go to the house. My grandmother's BMW sat in my driveway and I had the urge to make a run for it, but I knew she would make an appearance after the search. Her visits were sporadic, so I never knew when to expect her. She never called either. It was always a surprise.

I took a relaxing breath as I twisted the door knob, entering the kitchen. "Hey Nayna."

"Camille, this place is filthy. I wish you would hire an actual house keeper." She fluttered her hands around in the air then perched them on her narrow hips.

"I'm doing great by the way," I chirp as I toe off my boots.

"Get over here." She walks up to me, placing a diamond adorned finger on my chin to turn my head side to side. With squinted eyes she takes me in. "You look pale? Have you been sleeping? When's the last time you had an orgasm?"

Ladies and gentlemen, Patricia Harper.

I pull myself away from her grip. "Geez, Nayna. I'm fine. And for the one hundredth time, I'm not telling you anything about my sex life."

My nonexistent sex life, I mentally noted.

That's what you get when your grandmother is a sex/relationship therapist. I've been humiliated more than once by her questions and recommendations. She once even tried to "demonstrate" a new position at the PD Christmas party. I was traumatized to say the least.

She purses her lips as she glides over to the window to look out at the lake. "I heard you found something yesterday."

I reach into the cabinet to grab Achilles a treat. Anything to keep my hands moving. I knew what was coming next.

"Was that one of your little visions?" She asks.

Little visions.

"Wow."

She spins to face me, looking like ski resort barbie, decked out in her winter gear. It's not even snowing yet. "I'm not trying to be tacky dear…I just…you know your mother suffered from the same thing."

My nails dug into my palms. Any harder and I would be drawing blood. I hated when she talked about mom like that. Like she was *ill*.

She sighs and a flicker of remorse passes her face, but she straightens, and squares her shoulders. "You aren't doing anything to cause hallucinations are you, Camille?" She steps forward, sniffing me like a drug dog. "You haven't been experimenting with that devil's lettuce, have you?"

I nearly choked on my own spit. "Devil's what?" I coughed into my fist.

"You know," she waved her French tipped nails. "The Mar-I-Juan-a." She pronounced every syllable in a whisper

I snorted. "No Nayna, I haven't been smoking weed." I fed Achilles a treat. "And even if I did, it's completely legal now."

"I'm not judging dear." She used her hands to push my hair back over my shoulder. "I just don't want to give them any ammunition."

Nayna was good at heart. She loved me, but she had a hard time understanding me, just like she couldn't understand mom.

"Would you like a drink?" I offered.

"No thanks sweetie." She yanked on one sleeve of her coat. "Have you spoken to your sister."

"Which one?"

She rolled her eyes. "The one that deserted our family."

"Whitley went to college. She was literally here three months ago to visit."

My sister moved to California. It was a bold move and even though my father fought her tooth and nail, it was what she needed to do. I love my sister and even though it terrified me, I supported her.

Nayna flips her hair out from her coat and goes for the door. "I'll call you later to check in."

Yeah right. She whisks out the door, leaving a cold breeze blowing through my house that never seems to leave. Even though they all try not to show it, it's evident in their actions. I'm the daughter they have to worry about.

I'm the one with the whispers.

CHAPTER 15

Camille

I waved a hand in the air, flagging down Bekka and Tilly when they entered the diner. Elle and I sat at the back, tucked between two tables of loggers. They sat down, and I couldn't help but glance down at Bekka's ring finger that was still empty. Adam has had the ring for two weeks now. He's been waiting for the "right moment" and all this secrecy is absolutely killing me. I'm literally busting at the seams.

"Sorry we're late. The station is a madhouse," Bekka said as she plopped down across from Elle.

"What's going on?"

She unwrapped her pink scarf. "Nothing came from the air search. Now they are checking the surrounding area. Your dad had to kick out a reporter who somehow slithered his way in."

"Sounds eventful," Elle quipped.

"Yeah, then Easton and Dustin almost got into it. Adam had to hold him back. It almost got nasty." Bekka's eyes widened.

"Hmmp." Elle pretended to be uninterested and began spreading butter onto her roll.

She always acted that way where Easton was concerned.

Speaking of officers......I hear you have a new roomie. Tilly displayed an evil grin as her hands flared with an enthusiasm I didn't appreciate.

I narrowed my eyes at her. "Who told you?"

Adam.

"Well, I'm not happy about it," I announced.

"Why the hell not? He's a ten." Elle popped a piece of bread into her mouth.

"And he's rude," I added. I plucked my fork from the table and cut through one of the cheese sticks on the appetizer platter. "So now not only do I have a babysitter at the station, I have a live in babysitter at home."

"Oh, a babysitter! Does he give you a bath and tuck you in at night?" Elle wagged her eyebrows.

Bekka laughed and Tilly's shoulders silently shook. "He ain't bad to look at I'll give him that," Bekka admitted.

"That's not the point." I huffed.

"Then what is the point of this emergency lunch you called?" Bekka asked.

I ran a hand through my hair, and rested my elbow on the table. My eyes met Tilly's and I could see the empathy. She knew. She always knew.

Her hands lifted. *It's happening again?*

I nodded. "Yeah."

"When?" Elle asked as she reached out, squeezing my forearm.

"The night before her mom reported it." My eyes closed.

"Cami.... please don't do anything," Bekka started.

"She won't." Elle interjected. "She learned that the hard way."

I almost laughed, but it was true. I did learn the hard way.

Has it been just one dream? Tilly asked.

"Yeah just the one." I sighed. "Which led me to the scarf."

"You know we support you, Cam. No matter what," Elle reassured me.

"Thanks." I reached out and squeezed her hand.

"Just promise no solo late-night excursions." Bekka held out a pinky.

I gripped it with mine. "Promise. Don't worry, I won't get away with much as long as detective dick is breathing down my neck."

"I'd let him breathe down my neck," Elle said under her breath.

I released Bekka, elbowing Elle as we all busted out laughing. Even Tilly, which she quickly covered by her hands with flushed cheeks.

I knew Elle's comments where harmless, and I knew I most certainty did *not* like Jace Foster. So why did the thought of him being anywhere near Elle's neck make my stomach churn?

After lunch I spent the rest of the day doing my shopping for all of my cleaning supplies, some extra sheets, and some holiday décor. I loved getting the cabins prepared for Christmas. It was my absolute most favorite time of the year.

It was dark by the time I got home, and it took almost every ounce of strength I had to make it to the kitchen in one trip. I'd lose a limb before I made a second trip with any sort of shopping bag. With a groan I dropped all the bags onto the wooden floors and looked around the room. My hands propped on my hips when Achilles didn't greet me. The television was on, so I stepped around the bar and my feet almost stuck to the floor when I saw Jace relaxed on the couch with Achilles next to him. They were both focused on the football game playing on the big screen while Jace scratched along Achilles' neck.

"Well, what am I, chopped liver now?" I exclaimed to get his attention.

Achilles turned and he barked once before turning his attention back to the screen.

Jace smirked and slung an arm over the top of the couch.

"What kind of voodoo did you do to him?" I accused.

"I believe that's your area of expertise." He smiled arrogantly.

I almost threw him the bird, but he turned back to the TV. "I didn't do anything. We had a chat and now we're buds."

Shaking my head, I went back into the kitchen and put away all of the cleaning supplies. I had a small load of laundry to throw in, so I called out to Jace.

"You need anything washed?"

"Huh?" He shouted back.

I rolled my eyes as I hiked the laundry basket up under my arm. I walked back into the kitchen so I could peer through the cut out over the sink that overlooked the living room.

"I'm about to wash a load of clothes. It's small, so if you have anything that needs washing I'll toss it in."

He stood and I watched his lean body stride across my living room. He wore only a t-shirt and sweats which I preferred over his jeans. Then I scolded myself. Just because he's in the hot sweatpants club doesn't mean he's a good person. *He has zero manners.*

"I don't want you washing *my* clothes with your *dirty* underwear," he said as he glanced at the basket before picking up a glass on the counter.

I scoffed. "For your information detective, I don't wear underwear."

Whatever liquid he just ingested sputtered out and he coughed, pressing his hands flat against the granite. He coughed again and his face turned a very distinct shade of red.

"You, ok?" I asked as I took a step towards him.

He nodded and backed away from me. "I'm fine," he croaked out. He cleared his throat. "I'll wash tomorrow, you go ahead." Then without another glance, he disappeared up the staircase.

CHAPTER 16

Jace

I tried to think about something non sexual. Something so far away from the fact that I now know Camille Harper is bare at all times. *Think of old ladies. Bungee jumping. Sloths. Kittens. No.... not kittens.* I gave up. Sleep was almost nonexistent that night. I tossed and turned. On the plus side, I'm now up to speed on all mountain slang of northern Colorado. *I figured, when in Rome.*

I managed to survive my first week. I found myself not being as irritated with Camille's morning vocals and that in itself irritated me. I want to work. Do my job and not think about all the shit in my life that's blown up. Or think about her long legs every time I see her prancing around the kitchen. Or think about the four nights in a row I've woken to the sound of her crying in the middle of the night. I don't ask questions. She's all smiles the next day, so I mind my business. I ignore the urge to creep across the hall and check on her. I ignore the constant fucking urge to be in her vicinity.

It's Saturday. I've been burying myself in work, analyzing cold case after cold case that's gone nowhere. We are no further on Meredith's case than we were a week ago, so I reach for a file that I had printed that shows Camille's back ground. Does the captain know I ran a background check on his daughter? No. But I like to be thorough.

The sun had already gone down and I was nursing a beer. Camille was "sweeping the grounds" as she calls it. I'm assuming she means checking the cabins. I don't go with her. She deserves a little privacy.

I have all my folders out on the dining table since there's no desk in my room. It's been just me and Achilles for the last couple of hours. He sticks right with me when Camille is out. The back door opened, and a flushed Camille stepped inside. Her cheeks were red and she was frowning as she yanked off her scarf. Head lights came through the window and she peered out before muttering under her breath. The dining table isn't in view from the door, so she hadn't noticed me yet.

When a rapid fist beats on the door, I set my beer on the table and stand, stuffing my gun in the back of my jeans.

She forcefully tugged open the door, revealing a slender guy in a suit. He looks familiar, but I can't place him.

"Camille, answer your damn phone," he barks as he steps up to the threshold.

She moves into the doorway, blocking his entrance. "Why would I answer your call, Stuart?" She hisses.

"Come on. You know I miss you baby." He leans against the door jam, attempting to be sincere.

I can smell this guy's bullshit from here. The force will teach you that. Reading people.

"Stuart." She sighs. "I'm tired. I'm tired of you constantly pushing. It's over."

"But you aways say that.... then you end up back in my bed." He reaches a hand out to touch her hair and she swats it off.

That's my girl.

Wait, where the fuck did that come from?

My muscles flex as I try to stand still. He can talk all he wants, but he better keeps his hands to himself.

"I think it's best that you leave," she says as she wraps her arms around her waist.

I can tell she's uncomfortable. I don't like it.

He scoffs as he pushes off the door frame. "After all the shit you've pulled in this town? You think any man is going to want you?" He laughs. "You know damn well I'm the only one willing to set aside your issues."

She shakes her head, and before I even realize it, I'm on the move. This fucker is being disrespectful. I may be an asshole, but I would never downright manipulate someone.

"I believe she asked you to leave," I say as I step up behind Camille.

My chest hits her back and I feel her breath hitch. Stuart's eyes widen before he shifts them down to her, then back up to me.

"Who the fuck is this?" He asks, narrowing his eyes on her.

"Who the fuck are you?" I asked.

"Okay...it's time for you to go." Camille steps forward, but I reach out, wrapping my hand around her hip. I'm not sure what possessed me, but the look on his face was worth it.

I tugged her back against me. "It would be in your best interest to stay away from her," I warned.

I've got a couple inches on him, so I moved Camille behind me and I stood up straight, pinning him with my eyes to show just how serious I am.

"Oh, I see." He steps back, before an amused laugh filters from his mouth. "Just a fair warning, this one's crazy."

"Yet here you are." I shrug.

He steps off the porch and strides back to his overpriced SUV before he peels out of the driveway.

I shut the door behind me, turning to face Camille who is staring at me with wide eyes. "Thanks for that, but I can handle him," she finally says.

I ignore her comment and head back to my stack of people long forgotten by Timber Creek.

"You better watch yourself detective," she muses from behind me.

I take a seat, lifting my beer to my mouth. "Why's that?"

"For a second there you were tiptoeing the friendship line." She smiles as she places her elbows on the bar.

I take a swig before I land the bottle back down on the wooden table. "That was called work, Sunshine."

I inwardly cringe at the nickname. I call her that in my head, I've just kept it to myself. She laughs, tilting her head back, exposing the column of her throat. I have to look away to keep from picturing running my tongue across it.

"What's so funny?" I ask.

"You're probably the only person on the planet to refer to me as sunshine." She pushes off the bar, and reaches up, pulling the tie out of her hair, causing the blonde waves to fall down her back.

She laughs off my comment and I'm thankful, because I'm again reminding myself this is a job. I have no business calling her anything but her name. Hell, in all reality it should be Ms. Harper. Cut and dry.

Going back to my stack of Manila folders, I sift through and randomly grab the fourth one from the top. I'll go over her stuff later when I'm alone. This file isn't very thick, which tells me they didn't have much to begin with. I flip it open and my eyes scan the left page before I glance at the right.

I had just started to read the missing person's report when the piercing sound of shattering glass echoed behind me. I quickly haul to my feet, reaching for my gun, but when I see the source, I stall. Camille is standing in the middle of a pile of broken glass. Her lip's part and her eyes blink rapidly, filling with unshed tears.

"Camille?" I gently lay my gun down on the table.

Her blue eyes are honed in on the open folder. She's laser focused on the picture that's paper clipped at the top.

"Camille," I say again, a little harsher this time to get her attention.

She blinks, then shoots her gaze to mine. Her skin pales if that's even possible with how porcelain it is already and her hands begin to tremble.

"I'm so...ssssorry," she stutters out.

Her sock covered feet slide back and she hisses as she recklessly tramples the shards of broken glass.

"Stop," I order as I reach for her shoulders to steady her. "You're already bleeding."

I can see the blood soaking up the cotton material of her white socks. "I'm sorry, Jace." Her voice cracks and so does my resolve for a moment.

I reach down, scooping her up in my arms, then deposit her on the kitchen island.

"Don't move. Let me clean this up," I mumble.

She nods, still looking every bit as terrified as she was moments ago. She wasn't sunshine. She was consumed by the complete opposite.

Darkness.

CHAPTER 17

Camille

I can feel the chill of the granite through my thin leggings. I'm still in shock. Floored. I mindlessly tap a rhythm on the counter as I watch Jace sweep up the remaining parts of my tumbler. The pull to look over at the table is strong, but I fight it. The thud of my heart has not slowed. I close my eyes.

Blood. It's covering her green tank top.

It's real. She's real.

"Do you have a first aid kit?" Jace is now standing in front of me, his brows furrowed.

"Top of the cabinet in the bathroom." I almost don't even recognize my own voice.

I clear my throat as he takes the stairs two at a time.

Control your emotions, Camille.

I can practically hear my father's voice, something he's instilled in me. He says I'm too sensitive. Too quick to be influenced.

It's not real. They're just dreams.

The heavy thump of his boots brings me out of my thoughts. Jace's long legs eat up the space between the kitchen and living room.

"Take those socks off," he says as he flips open the first aid kit.

Even when he's doing something nice, he still figures out a way to be an ass.

I take a deep breath as I reach down, slipping my finger inside the fabric to remove my bloody socks. I toss them on the floor, then bring my leg up to inspect my heel.

"Don't touch the cuts," he says without even so much as a glance in my direction.

"Your bedside manner could use some work," I snapped.

His rough hands worked to open an alcohol wipe and a few packets of ointment along with two band aids. I focused on the movement. His fingers. His tan skin along his forearms. Anything to keep from thinking about the woman on my table. *The same woman. The same eyes.*

"Give me your foot." He motions his palm.

I narrow my eyes at him. When I don't immediately obey, his palm slides down my calf, before my heel lands in his hand. Tingles shoot up my leg at the heat of the contact. The touch isn't intimate. I know it's not. I can tell by the expression on his face, but it doesn't stop the dip in my stomach. He plants himself on the bar stool in front of me and rests my foot on his thigh.

"Are you gonna tell me what that was?" He asks as he lifts my ankle, swiping the cold cloth over my wounds.

"It was nothing." I wince at the burn.

He grunts. "That's a fucking lie."

My teeth clenched as he swiped over it again. "Considering we aren't even friends, I don't believe I owe you an explanation for anything, detective." He sat my foot down on his thigh and reached for the other. "Besides, I didn't think talking was your thing."

He continued to lightly clean my foot. It stung, but after the first few brushes the stinging subsided and it just felt cold. We spent the next few minutes in silence as he stewed over my last comment and continued to doctor my feet.

"Keep these bandaged tonight, then you can clean them in the morning," he rasped after he applied the last bandage.

I nodded as he stood, then gathered the empty packages and tossed them in the trash. When he stepped around the bar, my eyes caught on the blood that stained his jeans.

"Shit, Jace. Your pants," I said as I hoisted myself down from the counter top. "Let me clean those."

When I landed on my feet, I clenched the granite so hard my knuckles grew white. Pain. My tender soles ached as I took a few steps towards the laundry room.

"My pants are fine. You can barely walk," he said behind me.

"I'm ok." I waved a hand as I hobbled across the kitchen.

"Damn it, Camille," he grumbled and in a matter of three seconds I was spun around, and like a sack of potatoes I was slung over his broad shoulder.

"What on earth are you doing? Put me down!" I demanded.

He started towards the staircase and I saw Achilles lift his head and watch the entire thing go down without evening flinching. *Traitor.*

I hung like a rag doll as he climbed the stairs. "I don't believe this is part of your job," I sneered.

He ignored me, pushing open my bedroom door with ease like I weighed nothing, then with a quick jerk of his shoulder I was catapulted onto my bed. I bounced back and two of my pillows swallowed me up as I tried to gain my balance.

"Stay in bed," he said over his shoulder as he turned to leave.

"Don't order me around. I don't need your assistance or your pity," I spat.

He paused at my door and then he turned his sharp blue eyes on me. I swallowed as he assessed me. He squinted like he could read my every thought if he looked long enough.

"Get some rest. You look like you've seen a ghost."

My throat swelled at his word. Fear hit me all at once. Problem is, he's right on target. I did see a ghost. She's the first one I saw when I was sixteen years old.

And her picture it sitting on my dining room table.

CHAPTER 18

Jace

As if it's become a part of my morning routine, I lay in bed listening to Camille karaoke. You would think after practicing everyday it would improve, but the girl still can't carry a tune in a bucket.

I needed to get my run in before I started back with my case files, but as I lay here, all I can think about is *her*. If her feet are ok. *Her fucking feet.* I'm not a feet man. It's not my thing, but something switched in me last night and I felt the need to take care of her. They were so small and delicate compared to my giant hands and she looked terrified. Scared. It was ingrained in me to protect. It was my career. My passion. As much as I didn't want to give a shit, I did. My first thought as I heard her voice was wondering how she got down the stairs. Was it painful? I needed to check her bandages. *What the hell is wrong with me?*

"Not your job, Foster," I reminded myself as I rolled out of bed.

I tugged on some sweats and a hoodie, then my sneakers. I had gone on a few runs since I'd been here and I can admit it's peaceful. Quiet. When I run in town it's busy. The buzz of the locals and the lingering eyes of all the eligible bachelorettes make it hard to just get lost. I can get lost easily here. Get lost in the memories. The good times, not the bad ones.

When I jogged downstairs Camille smiled from behind her cup of coffee. She was wrapped up on the couch with Achilles tucked up next to her side, taking up the entire length as she scrolled through her iPad.

"Morning. Fresh coffee on the counter if you want any," she offered.

"Thanks." I reached for a mug and poured myself a cup, trying like hell to swallow the question burning on my tongue. Apparently, I didn't try hard enough. "How are your feet?"

I sipped my coffee casually, giving the illusion I was asking out of obligation instead of admitting the truth. *That I needed to know.*

"Better. I showered this morning and took off the bandages."

I nodded. And I guess since I was on a roll, I asked another dumb fucking question. "Who's Stuart?"

She paused her finger on the screen and glanced up at me. "He's my ex-boyfriend."

"He's a douche," I said before I took another sip.

"No argument there." She chuckled.

She sat aside her iPad and carefully raised up onto her feet, which I could tell were still sore by the uncomfortable face she made when she applied all of her weight. "Sorry about last night. He's a little…"

"Narcissistic?" I finished.

"Yeah..." She glanced down at her hands as a flush crept up her neck. "Sometimes I'm ashamed I let him manipulate me all those years." She cleared her throat. "He wasn't always like that."

Is she defending him?

I didn't know what to say. I wasn't someone who did feelings very well. Like now, how she looked at me like she would give anything for me to just talk to her. Talk to her about anything other than work. We talk about the case. That's as about as deep as it gets. As deep as I will allow it. *It's work.* Not play. Captain's orders.

And because I'm an asshole, I set my cup in the sink. "I'm going for a run. I'll be back."

Then I slipped out of the door before she could get out another word. I over stepped last night. It wouldn't happen again. I needed those release papers like I needed my next breath and even the blonde bottle of sunshine standing barefoot in the living room wasn't going to get in the way. I needed my life back on track. I needed things to go back to the way they were before I lost my best friend and was forced to step back from a job I loved. I needed some form of control back, and those papers gave me that. They gave me something to live for.

CHAPTER 19

Camille

It was Thanksgiving Day. We had aways held it at my parent's house and all of the PD came. Well, the ones that weren't on duty. We would take plates and drop them off at the precinct for those on the clock. I had to get there early to cook. Tilly was meeting me there and Whitley was flying in at 10:00. Adam was picking her up and I was so excited to have all of my family under one roof.

I tugged on my knee-high boots and gave one last glance back at the mirror before I trotted down the stairs. I paused when I saw Jace in his sweats, watching tv.

"Hey..." I said as I leaned against the wall dividing the rooms. "Are you coming to dinner tonight? Or are you going to see your family?"

"No, my brother is out in L.A. and my mom just moved to North Carolina with my stepdad. We haven't really spent holidays together in years." His attention was still held on the tv and his voice held almost zero emotion. *Per usual.*

"I'm sorry." It made my heart ache to hear that. I cherished the holidays with family. Even more so now that we have to get through them without mom. I pulled my keys from my purse. "You can come to my dad's. The whole office will be there. It's tradition."

"Thanks for the invite."

He still never tuned to face me. So, I finally grabbed my bag of ingredients I had on the counter and headed into town.

⁂

The holiday spirit was in the air. So was the smell of the turkey in the oven, the scent of apple pie, and I was just beginning to prepare the pumpkin rolls. I just needed my little helper.

"When's June coming?" Tilly asked.

I smiled when she used her voice instead of her hands. She only did it when she felt comfortable. Safe. She always felt safe in our childhood home.

"She should be here any minute." I dusted the flour off of my hands and wiped them on my apron just as the doorbell rang. "That's probably her!"

I passed by Bekka who gave me a pleading look that said *rescue me* as Nayna had her cornered in the dining area. All I heard was "healthy" and "breath play" and I almost tripped over my own feet.

Before I could get to the door a head of brown curls was barreling towards me. "Cami!!" She squealed.

"Hey there June bug." I wrapped the toddler in my arms and lifted her off of her feet.

"She's been up since 6:00." Easton scrubbed a hand down his face.

"Sorry," I apologized.

He chuckled. "It's fine. As long as she's smiling, I'm happy."

"Knock knock!" Elle's voice came from behind Easton and he stepped aside to let her through the door.

"Ellie!!!!" June scrambled down from my arms and the second her little feet hit the floor she was charging towards her.

"Good morning sweet girl." Elle bent to her knees and embraced her tiny little body.

Emotions swelled in my throat. I don't know how anyone could leave such a precious girl behind. But I've known Savanah since we were kids and she's one of the most self-centered people I've ever met, so I guess it's not a huge shock she didn't put her own child before herself. But it wasn't just the embrace that had me swallowing over the lump in my throat. It was the look on Easton's face.

"Are we ready to bake?" I asked, trying to break the tension.

"Yes!" June wiggled out of Elle's arms and yanked on her hand. "Cook with me Ellie."

They took off and I walked over to close the door behind Easton.

"I'll be back in a few hours. Gotta get ready for Grey's game," he said as he opened the door to his truck.

I waved and closed the door behind me. Greyson was Easton's older brother who was in the NFL and played football for San Antonio. He was practically a celebrity in this town, but to us, he was just *Grey*. I started for the kitchen, but caught sight of a picture on the table in the foyer. My hand reached out to touch the gold frame. Honey eyes and blonde hair smiled back at me. *Mom*. I wish she was here. I wish I would have known……and I wish I could have saved her.

A tear slowly slid down my cheek just as the front door opened. My eyes met my sister's and she dropped her bag on the floor.

"None of that, Camille Harper." She pointed her finger like the boss babe she was.

God, I missed her.

"Hey Whit." I sat down the frame and met her halfway across the foyer where she squeezed me like she hadn't seen me in years.

"I missed you," I said.

"I'm your favorite sibling, what do you expect?" She pulled back and winked before slipping around me to address the girls in the kitchen that were shouting her name.

I smiled to myself. Thanksgiving was finally about to be in full swing.

CHAPTER 20

Jace

It was close to five. I knew kick off was soon because I was now a part of the group text between Easton, Adam, and Rex. In the past I was usually working on Thanksgiving, but if I wasn't, I would go with Natalie to her family's place in New York. I never enjoyed it. A lot of rich people talking about how much money they had and questioning when I was going to marry their daughter. Maybe that's why I asked her. Who knows. Peer pressure? The next step. Whatever, it's over now.

Easton: Foster your ass better be here. June and Cami worked really hard on those pumpkin rolls.

Me: You act like they made them just for me.

Easton: They did. June said it was a present for my new friend.

Well shit.

Adam: Cami's pumpkin rolls are legendary.

Rex: Which is why I'm going to marry her.

I tossed my phone down and glanced around the room. Screw it. I had nothing better to do.

Cap's house was filled with chatter when I stepped through the door. Bekka, Elle, Tilly, and another girl I didn't recognize were in the kitchen, stacking plates and preparing dishes. Cap stood behind the couch that was occupied by Adam and Easton, and a very excited little girl who sat on her dad's shoulders. Rex was on his feet, pacing the living room. It was barely half way through the first quarter and he was already sweating.

I took a few more steps when I almost bumped into someone coming around the corner. *Sunshine.*

"Jace…" She looked up at me and stepped back. "You came." She smiled.

I shrugged. "Don't get too excited."

She rolled her pretty eyes. "I'm never excited to see you."

"Is that so?" I dipped my hands into my pockets.

I watched the blush hit her cheeks as she glanced away then back to me.

What the hell are you doing, Foster? Flirting with the captain's daughter? In his own kitchen?

"Dinner is almost ready. The guys are watching the game." She pointed to the couch before she joined the women in the kitchen who all seemed to have stopped their conversation to watch our interaction.

"Hey Jace," Bekka called out and I gave a nod as I passed to join the group in the living room.

"Foster." Captain Harper shook my hand and I stood next to him behind the couch.

"You watch unkey Grey?" June asked with a tilt of her head.

I chuckled. "Yeah, I'm here to watch the game."

She studied me, scrunching her tiny nose.

"Hey man." Easton turned and patted June's leg. "June, this is my friend, Jace."

Her eyes bugged out. "You bossy to Cami." She crossed her arm.

My eyes cut to the kitchen. So, someone's been talking shit.

"Cami is the bossy one." I leaned down. "She told me I *had* to eat one of those pumpkin rolls you made."

She smiled and clapped her hands.

"Alright! Who's ready to eat!" A woman with light brown hair who shared similar features to Adam stood at the opening of the living room.

If I had to guess, this is the other Harper sister. She assessed me from head to boot before clapping her hands. "Everybody up!"

All the guys stood immediately. *Bossy seems to run in the family.* We circled around the dining table, and the guys removed their hats. Camille stood next to me, and Rex landed on my other side.

"I'm going to say Grace, then we can dig in," Cap announced.

Everyone started to join hands and my pulse quickened. Camille was next to me. I had to touch her. *Again.* It was already too much to touch her damn feet, now I have to hold her hand. I kept my face neutral and held my hand out. She looked at my open palm for a moment before she schooled her face just the same, then laid her soft skin on mine.

"You gonna hold my hand or what, Foster?" Rex smirked.

I glared at him as I grabbed his hand, squeezing just hard enough he cursed under his breath. "Geez. You don't have to be so violent."

Ignoring him, my attention was brought back to the silky skin that wrapped around me. Her hand felt so small against mine. I held on loosely as Cap began the prayer. My body felt hot. My hand even hotter the longer our skin was fused together. The words spoke out loud started to fade and all I could focus on was this feeling. Whatever it was. I'm not sure when my body decided to betray me, but my fingers lifted on their own, rotating just enough that she had no choice but to let go. I spread out my fingers, giving her access to intertwine her fingers with mine. Which she did, like it was natural. Like we'd held hands a million times and this was a normal transition. When they clasped together again my thumb moved, brushing across her knuckles. I snuck a quick peek to her face. Her eyes were closed, but her lips parted when I brushed her knuckles again. As if she felt the weight of my gaze, her eyes flash open and moved to mine.

"Amen!" Cap boomed.

"Amen" was repeated throughout the room and I immediately released Rex's hand. But the other, the one that held onto the sunshine lingered. It lingered until a throat cleared and we both jerked away.

My eyes met Easton's and he gave me a look that asked *what the fuck are you doing?*

Believe me, I wish I knew.

CHAPTER 21

Jace

Another week had passed, where I went back and forth about the updates of the case and tried to avoid Camille as much as I could. I was starting to wake up hoping she was downstairs when I got coffee, and that set off all my fucking alarms. My rent house couldn't be ready soon enough.

Adam, Easton, and Rex were watching Greyson's game tonight, so I spent a few hours laughing at Rex's lame jokes. Captain said I could use a break, and apparently the girls wanted a girl's night, so I was relieved of my babysitting duties for the evening. She didn't need me. I'm not sure why that notion pisses me off. It's not like I even like her. I don't like her for a specific reason. I don't like that I find myself listening for her voice when I wake up. I don't like the fact my eyes drift to her ass when she wears those tight leggings and I sure as hell don't like how I think of her lips when my hand travels south in the shower. *I really need to find a fuck buddy. A Brunette preferably.*

After the Chiefs ended the game with a win, I drove back to the cabin. It was starting to get colder and I knew the first heavy snow wasn't too far away. The entire place was quiet when I pulled up. Just the full moon above the still lake. Two cars were parked by Camille's jeep, so I knew the girl's night wasn't over yet.

As I walked up to the door, I heard a loud screech followed by a shriek of laughter. Music was playing, but even through the thump of the bass I knew it was Camille and I quickened my steps. I stepped through the frame and took two strides across the kitchen when I froze. There she stood, in front of the tv in nothing but a white sports bra and skin tight white leggings. *Fuck me.* She rotated her hips, bending slightly at the waist as her hands trailed up her sides, then she laughed again, head tilted back causing all that blonde hair to water fall down her spine. The person on the tv gave the next command and she lifted her hands above her head, and followed the instructions.

"You got a flashlight in there or just happy to see Camille?" A feminine voice came from my right.

I glanced over to Elle, who was followed by Bekka. She was wearing something similar to Camille, but all her dark hair was pulled up on top of her head. I immediately turned, pressing my apparent hard on against the bar. "What the hell are y'all doing?"

"Dirty dancing." She smiled before taking a sip from her bottle of water. "It's therapeutic."

"Is there any more wine?" A raspy voice came from the laundry room then Tilly rounded the corner.

Her eyes widened and she lowered her head in embarrassment. I didn't know she spoke so well. I've only seen her sign. She actually had a really cool voice. She uncomfortably shifted on her bare feet, then signed what I'm assuming was "hey". I don't really know sign language, so I wasn't sure how to understand her.

"Hey Tilly." I waved.

"Jace! Come dance!" Camille shouted from the living room.

Elle laughed. "She might be a little drunk."

Camille proceeded to bend completely over as her palms landed on the couch and she swung her hips again. I had to stifle a groan that lodged in my throat. "No thanks."

"You don't want to dirty dance with me?" Camille stood up straight, then hiccupped.

For fucks sake.

"It looks like detective Foster had a *hard* day. He's probably ready to hit the sheets." Elle's smirk stretched across her face as she joined Camille in the living room.

"Fine, I didn't want to dance with you anyway. You're always so grumpy." Camille's hair fell across her face as she plopped down on the couch. "He never wants to talk and he doesn't even like it when I put those beautiful flowers by his bed. I handpicked those, Elle," she slurs.

"Okay, Cami. I think that's enough dirty dancing for one night." Elle reached down to yank her up, giving me an apologetic look.

"Yeah, it's time to go. Load up Tilly," Bekka called out as she slipped on her coat.

"And you know what?" Camille attempts to whisper, but I can still hear every word as I turn my back and head for the stairs. "The flowers...I picked those because they match his eyes. Aren't his eyes pretty?"

My shoulders flinch.

"So blue.... but so sad," she says quietly.

I pause at the top of the stairs, waiting for anything else to fall from her lips. But it's quiet, so I step into my room, walking directly over to the flowers next to my bed. The flowers I've barely even noticed. I touch the soft petals as my chest pinches.

They don't just match my eyes.

They match hers.

CHAPTER 22

Camille

For the first time in a long time, I stood in front of my bathroom mirror. Drunk. I usually didn't drink. But considering the other night when I saw those hollow eyes stare back at me from a case file, it seemed like a given. I stared at the prescription bottle in my hand, debating pouring them down the drain, but instead I sat it back in the cabinet next to my face cream. I was prescribed those sleeping pills a few years ago, but I don't want to take them. I don't want to miss anything. It's been years. Years since I've seen her in my dreams. I *knew* something had happened to this woman. But at the time I didn't understand it. When the dreams didn't end, I tried to convince everyone else, then that's when the more delusional I appeared. It was the first time they ever came to me. *His first victim.*

I splashed cold water on my face before turning out the light and tiptoeing to bed. I pulled the plush comforter up under my arms and I waited. I waited for sleep to come. And I waited for *her*. I waited for Meredith to give me anything, something to show me where she was. This time I was determined to find her for before it was too late.

I blink open my eyes. It's morning, the sun is shining and a feeling of disappointment washes over me. She never came. I lean up, bringing my fingers to my temples as I roll out of bed. She hasn't given me anything in a week. If I do dream it's the same one. The one with her scarf. *I have that, Meredith. I need something else.*

That whole bottle of wine I had last night has caught up with me and my head pounds with every step I take down the stairs. I fill up a glass of water, gulping it down as I glance out across the lake. I can see Jace on the other side, out for his morning run. My heart rate increases. I haven't been able to get down to the cellar all week with him right on my heels. I take another gulp and place my cup in the sink before I tug on my coat and sneak out the door.

I grip the small key that's in my coat pocket as I walk around the side of the cabin. I unlock the door as I peek over my shoulder and slip inside, taking the steps down into the cellar. A thin rope hangs from the ceiling and I yank it so the light turns on. My feet carry me to the desk, and I pick up a brown file. I managed to stash it down here before I was assigned a freaking bodyguard. There's not much here on Meredith. Just the basics. Name, address, birthday. The report from her mother and a recent picture. I swallow as I look at it. She's wearing a pink sweater. The same one from my dream. I lift my eyes to the large bulletin board I have hung on the wall. Three pictures line the top, and underneath are the details of their disappearance. Three women. Three women I've dreamed of being taken.... three women who have never been found.

The woman I saw in Jace's folder, she was the first one I dreamed of. I didn't understand it at the beginning, and I was confused when I saw her picture plastered all over the news. My dad had shut me down when I tried to tell him about my dream. I brushed it aside. It was a coincidence. But when the second happened......I tried even harder to convince them. But they didn't believe me. My dad and Nayna agreed I needed "help". Hence the two years of therapy and a multitude of medications. Everyone at the station saw my outburst when I pleaded with my father, and word only spread from there. If only my mom would have been there. She would have understood me. She would have believed me.

I'm lost in the report when the door slams upstairs. The file drops to the floor, causing the papers to loosely scatter over the concrete. I curse, bending down to gather them quickly. I don't want Jace to see any of this. Last thing I need is my father finding out I've been obsessed and doing my own investigation on the side. I shove the papers back in and set the file back on the table before I scramble back up to the yard.

I right my hoodie, and glance down, realizing I'm not wearing any pants.... or underwear. *Great.* I roll my shoulders back, acting completely natural as I glide through the front door. In my attempt to appear invisible, I kept my eyes on my mud boots, but that backfired when I smack right into a solid chest.

"Shit, sorry," Jace says as his hands reach out to my upper arms. "Where the hell were you?"

"Oh, I uh...was checking my Christmas decorations down in the cellar." I smile and nervously tuck a piece of hair behind my ear.

He frowns, glancing down at my bare legs.

I nod, a little excessively. "Sorry. I forgot pants."

I step around him, jogging towards the stairs as normal as possible. When I peek back over my shoulder, he's staring at me. More specifically, at my bare ass.

Chapter 23

Jace

This had been the longest day of my entire life. After seeing Camille this morning, I had to remove myself from the premises and do anything I possibly could to remove the image of her naked ass from my brain. I figured looking at a bunch of crime scene photos would be the answer. *I was fucking wrong.*

I made it up to my room, but figured I better return Adam's call before I hit the shower.

When he answered, I didn't even bother with a greeting. "Any luck with the security footage?" I reach behind me, tugging my shirt over my head.

"All we could see was her walking out and to the side of the building. No cameras on that side. All we know is she left at 11:00am," Adam says with a sigh. "I feel like we don't have a fucking thing. No signal from her phone, no credit card use, no social media use. It's like she..."

"Dropped off the face of the earth," I finish.

"Yeah," he huffed. "Dad is pissed. The ex isn't talking and the mother shows up every day demanding answers."

I sat down on the edge of my bed.

"Sorry man," he apologized. "I'm ranting. How's Camille? Anything happening out there?" He asks.

"No. Nothing new."

Nothing but me pretending I didn't notice her naked ass as she climbed the stairs this morning.

"But she's good?" He asks again.

I shrug. "I guess. It's not like we have girl talk over mimosas."

"You're such a dick, Foster." He chuckles. "I know she's a handful. Have you heard her sing yet?"

I bark out a laugh. "It's fucking awful."

"Try being forced to be in a band with her at age eight. I was the drummer." He deadpans. "She was the lead singer."

I chuckle as he turns serious. "She's quirky, but she's one of the best people I've ever known. Keep her safe, Jace."

"You have my word," I promised before ending the call.

I had almost dozed off when the silence was struck with a strangled cry. My eyes flew open and I darted upright. The cry rang out again, intertwined with a scream. I jumped out of bed, sliding my legs into the nearest set of sweats and I was out the door. My skin prickled as I crossed the hallway, closer to Camille's cries. I've always had a protective instinct, but it's never been this strong. Not with anyone else. Not with someone I don't even want to like.

With my fists clenched, I pushed open her door, charging straight forward to her bed. My eyes searched the dark, looking for an intruder, but nothing else was in the room. Just her, crowded against her head-board as she gasped for air. Her chest heaved as her hands frantically tugged at her oversized shirt. She cried out again, her eyes widening as tears spilled out over her cheeks.

"Camille," I called, hoping she could hear me.

"No." She spoke hoarsely. "Don't take her."

She cried out again, and I couldn't handle it. My knees hit the mattress as I reached out for her. She was having a nightmare that she seemed desperate to get out of, so I clamped my hands down onto her wrist.

"Camille," I said, softer this time.

She sucked in a heavy breath and her eyes gravitated to mine. I used my thumbs to rub small circles on her wrists. "It's just a dream. It's not real." Her back pressed against the headboard and she gasped again. "It's not real," I reiterated.

Her mind must have evaded the dream, because more tears over flowed as she croaked out my name. "Jace."

Pushing off of her bare feet, she lunged forward, wrapping her arms around my neck. She pressed into me, quivering from head to toe as she sobbed into my neck. I flexed my fingers, my hands held wide, as far away from her as possible. *I wasn't supposed to touch her. I didn't need to touch her.*

She squeezed tighter. "You're real."

My arms dropped in surrender, winding around her waist as I crushed her to my chest. "I'm real, Sunshine."

Her face stayed buried in the crook of my neck, while one of my hands held the back of her hair and the other slid up and down her back in a smooth pattern. After a few minutes, I was aware this position was compromising. Her legs were around my waist, but I couldn't let go. I held on until the sobs that wracked her body disappeared, then I gently laid her back under the covers.

Her cheeks were red and her eyes swollen. My fingers traced her jaw as I took in her features. Her brow pinched like she was still seeing something she didn't approve of. I remembered what she had said to me. *I didn't ask for this.*

It wasn't my job. But I knew right then if she ever had another nightmare, I would be right there to hold her. It didn't matter that she was the captain's daughter, or that I had the voice in the back of mind that warned me I was getting too close, getting attached, which was something I made sure to never do. That's the last thing I needed. But I was starting to realize...... Camille Harper was something I *wanted*.

CHAPTER 24

Camille

I can still feel his hands. The hardness of his chest. The gentle strokes down my back. I saw an entirely different Jace last night. One that was kind, soothing, and warm. Nothing like the cold as steel attitude he's given me since we met. It's comforting and terrifying at the same time. In that moment all I wanted was his arms. His voice that whispered *sunshine* in my ear. But it was a moment. Just one. Because this morning as I drink my coffee on the couch, staring out at the snow-covered ground, I know he'll be back to "detective". Not my friend. Not anything. Just the man who's forced to be here. Paid to be here.

Last night was different. I've never had a dream that vivid. A dream where I could smell the dampness of a musty room. Feel the terror radiating from someone else's eyes. Like I was connected to them. Tethered together so I felt every single feeling she did. *Meredith.*

I close my eyes. This time it was a necklace. I know I've seen it before. The room was dark, but that necklace was clear as day. I could see every detail. *It seemed familiar.* Movement outside caught my eye. It was Jace, running in the snow, headed to the other side of the lake.

Perfect.

I snuck outside. My boots sank into our first layer of snow for the season as I descended down into the cold cellar. It reminds me of the life these women have found themselves in. Somewhere cold. Empty. Dark. I take advantage of the small window of time. The necklace is still fresh in my mind and I know I've seen it somewhere. Pulling open my lap top, I search for local jewelry stores and scan the selections. *Nothing.* Nothing resembling the silver cross pendent.

Where have I seen that?

I chew on my lip and try to transfer myself back to the dream. She couldn't breathe. She was gasping. The only thing I could see was the necklace. Right in front of my eyes.

What are you showing me, Meredith?

I knew it was time. But with all the movement within the station I had to be careful. I had met with every one of these women's parents. They all spoke so highly of their daughters. My heart went out to them at their brokenness. The not knowing. The need for closure. Of all the parents I spoke with there was one similarity. One component that tied all of them together to give me the audacity to make my assumption. My theory. Every single missing woman went missing in public. In the middle of town without raising any suspicions. I knew it in my gut.

He was from Timber Creek. And I probably already knew him.

It was someone they felt safe with. Someone they trusted. Someone they would never question.

"Well look at that." A gruff voice breaks my trance.

I spin around in my chair to see Jace with his arms crossed and an eyebrow raised.

"What are you doing down here?" I jump up, shutting my lap top in the process.

"I think the better question is what are you doing?" He motions a hand to my bulletin board. "What the fuck is all of this?"

"It's nothing." I walk towards him, but he brushes past me.

He casually walks over, scanning the pictures and notes I've written over the last couple of years.

"Jace, please."

"Does your father know about this?" He glances over his shoulder at me.

"No and I would appreciate if you would keep this to yourself." I rush over, attempting to move him aside so I can pull down the sheet that covers it when I know I'm having guests.

He reaches out, catching me by the crook of my elbow. "Camille. What is this all about?" He studies the pictures again. "One of these is a cold case."

"Well, someone has to find these girls." I yank my arm away. "He's taking them, Jace. He has been for years. I told you that."

"Who?" He frowns.

"I don't know!" I shout. My hands run through my hair. "I just..."

"Wait...so you've been doing all of this for *years*?"

I look away, not wanting to see the judgments in his eyes.

"I don't even want to know how you obtained half of this information. I know your dad didn't hand it over."

"I have connections."

"I thought he didn't want you doing anything outside the station on your own?" He shakes his head. "We need to know if you..."

"No! You can't tell him!" I take his bicep in my grip. "Please, Jace. I can't go through it again. They don't believe me."

"Believe what?" He takes a step towards me. His large body towers over me, and at the most inconvenient moment I feel heat between my legs. I'm thinking of the way his arms wrapped around me last night, not the fact one slip of his tongue could obliterate me. *In a multitude of ways.*

"Nothing."

He lifts a brow. "Believe what?"

I lower my eyes, focusing on the toe of his Nike sneakers. "You'll just think I'm crazy."

A small chuckle leaves his lips. "Sunshine, I already think your crazy."

It takes all my strength to look him in the eye. The blue eyes that match my flowers. I take a deep breath, and prepare to give him a part of me only a few people know.

"I've had these dreams since I was sixteen.."

I see his jaw loosen, like that wasn't a surprise. Of course, he's not surprised. He witnessed that shit show already.

It's my next words that leave the heavy silence. "I think the person taking these women is in law enforcement."

CHAPTER 25

Jace

I'm assuming my face shows exactly my reaction about what she just said.

"See!" Her hands wave around in the air. "You think I'm crazy! I can see it all over your face."

"So, you're saying because of these dreams, you are accusing a man of the law to be responsible?" I scrub a hand across my jaw.

"Of course, you put it like that." She jerks on the sleeves of her sweater. "You don't believe me. Just like everyone else." She laughs, but it's halfhearted. "And you're going tell my father because it's pretty clear you hate me."

I can see the moisture fill her eyes. *Damn it.*

"Camille," I start.

"Don't even deny it, Jace. You avoid me. If we do speak it's like pulling teeth for more than a two-word response." She moves past me and raises up on her toes, letting the grey sheet fall over the pictures.

"Camille," I say again.

She's muttering to herself as she stomps to the other side of the cellar to gather a few papers on top of the desk.

I want to say she's full of it. Crazy, maybe even unhinged, but I saw it with my own eyes. I saw the fear last night. It was real to her.

"Sunshine." I try next.

She freezes, then turns to face me. Two tears streak down her flushed cheeks and it damn near cracks my heart. Well, the remaining elements of it.

"I don't hate you. I'm here to protect you." I take a deep breath. "And I want you to tell me. Tell me about your dreams."

She swipes a tear away and rolls her shoulders back. "Fine." She moved forward, brushing right up against me as she stormed to the door. "Are you coming, detective?" She snaps over her shoulder.

"Right behind you."

I walk behind her into the living room. She kicks off her boots and I slide out of my running shoes that are damp from the snow. She doesn't speak, but goes directly to the fridge, pulling out milk, eggs, some butter, and then heads to the pantry. I watch in silence. Tracking every movement. I watch the sway of her hair, the way her lips purse, and how her small hands move everything in its place. She's beautiful. One of those women who are one of a kind. She can't be *my* woman. Not that I want one. I already gave up on that life a long time ago, but I'd be lying if I said I wasn't curious about what's beyond the cashmere sweater she seems to favor.

She clears her throat. "I had my first dream when I was sixteen." She pulls a bowl out from under the counter. "I thought it was just a bad nightmare. One time thing." She pauses, and her eyebrows raise. "Why are you just sitting on your ass?" Bending down again, she brings up two aprons. "Get this on and get to work."

"I'm not wearing a fucking apron," I scoff.

"Then I'm not telling you anything." She tosses one at me as if she already knows I'm going to cave.

And I do. Because something about her being this honest with me makes me feel for her. I know what it's like when someone wants you to share the deepest parts of yourself. The parts you keep hidden.

I push to my feet, tying this ridiculous white apron around my waist as I do.

"Perfect." She smiles.

"What do you want me to do?" I ask. "I'm not much of a baker."

"Measure out 2¾ cup of milk and get two eggs."

I begin to do as she asks as she continues on. "Two days later a woman went missing. My dreams never show distinct facial features. Mostly the eyes, but I can always see what they're wearing. I saw her on a poster, and just thought it was weird. They ended up saying she ran off. She was young and wild, and they could never prove foul play."

I poured the milk into a bowl, then cracked an egg.

"The second dream happened two years after that one. Same dream just different woman." She reaches across me, snatching up the measuring cups. The bottom of her breast drags across my arm and I almost cracked my jaw I clenched it so hard. "This time when she was reported missing five days later, I paid attention."

"You told your dad?" I ask.

Her shoulders tense. "Yes. And he thought it was hormones or my imagination. I wasn't resting well, or whatever other excuse he could come up with." She shook her head. "My mom had recently passed, so he thought I was seeking attention. I was sent to a therapist and put on meds for anxiety and depression. Turns out therapy is what fucked me up more than anything."

I guess I understand why he would be concerned. From a cop's perspective.

"Whisk this, please." She handed me a silver apparatus and I began "whisking".

"When the third happened. I tried to warn him. I pleaded with him to see this wasn't accidents, or just another woman who went into the mountain and didn't come home. I tried everything to keep it from happening again."

I feel my hands clench around the metal. She must have been young. The thought of her being treated like that makes my blood rush.

"Anyway.... I stopped telling him after that. I lie to them about my pills. I don't take them. I hate the way they make me feel. All I want to do is prevent this man from taking them. I just want to save them."

I stop, placing the cooking utensil on the granite. "Do you see him?"

She stops and glances up at me. "Just his hands."

I see the look in her eye. Every single word out of her mouth is the truth. It's her truth. Now, whether I believe it or not is my prerogative. But *her*. It's real to her.

And now I'm not sure what to do with it, or what to do with this weird feeling.

CHAPTER 26

Camille

Three hours later we had made pancakes, waffles, blueberry muffins, and I had just stashed a peach cobbler in the oven. After my big confession we worked alongside each other in comfortable silence.

"This could be some good blackmail," I pointed out as I turned to see him with my white lace apron tied around his waist as he cleaned a mixing bowl in the sink.

Seeing him in nothing but a pair of jeans the first time we met was hot, but this, this broody man cleaning in my kitchen.... I shook away the thought. He wasn't here for my ogling. He was here to make sure I didn't do anything stupid. Maybe Elle was right. *I needed some...*

"I will be checking your phone tonight," he stated.

I laughed just as his phone buzzed on the counter. His hands were still in the sink, so he asked me to check it. *Hailey* flashes across the screen. A nauseating feeling hit me out of nowhere.

"It's Hailey. Do you need to get it?" I asked.

He immediately stiffened at the name. "No. It's fine."

I watched him. He roughly scrubbed the bowl, then sat it on the drying wrack before he was ripping off the apron. He reached around me for his phone and shoved it into his pocket.

Was that his girlfriend? *Oh my god. He has a girlfriend and I was in his lap.....with my legs....*

"Is she your girlfriend?" The question was out of my mouth before I could stop it. "I don't.... I don't want her to be uncomfortable with us staying in the same house together."

His hand planted on the bar and his shoulders hunched. "No, she's not. I told you I don't do girlfriends."

"Oh, okay. I mean.... well, if y'all are..."

"We aren't anything," he snapped.

"Jesus, Jace." I tossed a dirty spoon into the sink and the sound made him flinch. "You don't have to bite my head off. God forbid you tell me anything about your life after I practically laid myself out on a freaking silver platter for you."

He sighed and tilted his head back. I crossed my arms, waiting.

"It's my ex-partner's wife.... or widow," he finally said.

Widow. That means his partner.....the shooting.

"I'm sorry," I whispered.

He shook his head and eased down on the bar stool. "I haven't spoken to her since the funeral. Waylon was my best friend...and I just." He ran a rough hand through his dark hair. "I don't know what to say." He barked out a dry laugh. "He had a fucking family. A new baby and I had.... nothing."

I walked over closer to him. I could tell he was struggling. In the little time I've known him I've figured out he avoids anything remotely close to actual emotions.

"Every time I think about him I just wish it would have been me. I had nothing to live for and he had everything," he admitted.

I reached out, wrapping my fingers around his wrist. "You can't do that to yourself."

"I should have stopped him." I could feel his pulse racing. "I told him to hold back, but when he took off, I hesitated. I waited and it cost him his life. I was trained better than that. *I am* better than that."

"That's a pretty big burden to put on yourself."

"Yeah, well now she's having the burden of losing her husband and being a single mother."

His eyes lowered, focusing on my fingers that attempted to circle his wrist. "She's an officer's wife. She knows the risks. She loved him anyway knowing at any moment he could be taken from her."

I tried to give him something to cling to. Words to help him let go of the guilt. But that's all I had was words. I wanted to wrap him up like he did to me. But that wasn't what we were.... hell, we weren't even friends.

His eyes moved from my grip, then up to my face. I felt their caress and then a small smirk tilted his lips.

His free hand reached up. "You have some flour..."

His thumb gently swiped across my bottom lip. Slow, with just enough pressure to make me lose my breath. It was a reaction to let my tongue slide out to moisten them and he swallowed thickly at the act. The first level of my cabin was a decent size. But with every second that ticked by I felt the walls closing in. My chest felt tight and that familiar heat traveled between my legs.

He stood, causing me to shuffle back until my back hit the counter behind me. He followed, using his arms to cage me in against the cabinets. I wasn't sure what he was about to do, but I had a war going on inside me. I desperately wanted him to kiss me, but I also wanted him to say something hateful. Something to remind who he was. An asshole. Men like him didn't want the same things I did. Commitment. Family. Monogamy.

"I'll keep your secret, Sunshine." His breath fanned across my forehead. "If you keep mine."

I chanced a glance up to his face, which was a terrible idea. His eyes burned with want. *Need.* It was clear as day and I looked off to the side in case mine revealed the same. I wasn't stupid. I knew the hands off rule my father had with all the guys down at the station. I knew the consequences.

"What's your secret?" I asked, barely above a whisper.

He leaned down, just close enough to brush against the shell of my ear. "I don't hate you. Not even a little bit."

Then he pushed off the counter and disappeared up the stairs. I sagged against the cabinet as the truth slammed into me.

I didn't hate him either. Not even a little bit.

CHAPTER 27

Camille

It had been a long day. I had planned to go into the station, but apparently the group of kids in cabin three thought it would be a good idea to play golf. Inside the master bedroom. So now I've been dealing with window shopping and pleading with Curtis, our handyman, to come replace it before the newest guests arrive. It didn't help I had to visit three different stores before I was able to find a matching one. Who knew windows were so hard to come by, so by the time the evening had rolled around I was done for. I was nestled on the couch with a glass of wine and Achilles was curled up by the fire. The evening was quiet and I was even able to forget about the way I felt last night in the kitchen. Forget the way my body crackled with electricity at his closeness. That was, until he walked in the front door. I didn't take my eyes off of the television. I waited to see where he would go. If he would come in here with me, or retreat to his room like usual. I wasn't sure if I was disappointed, or thankful when he went upstairs. I relaxed against the cushions and sipped my wine. I didn't need him down here anyway. Distance was best.

My favorite part of the movie in *Good Will Hunting* had just finished when I got a whiff of cologne. Jace stood at the entry way of the living room with jeans, a white t-shirt, bare feet, and a beer in his hand. His hair was slightly rustled like he'd been running his hand through it in frustration all day. Which wouldn't surprise me.

"Long day?" I asked.

He took a pull from his beer before he entered the room, then sat on the chair closest to the fire. *And farthest from me.*

"Yeah." He sighed.

"Anything new on Meredith?"

He shook his head. "No. They had some DNA on the scarf. Her's and an unknown male. No matches in the system."

"I figured they wouldn't even run that," I said before I took another drink.

"I asked them to." He lowered his beer, balancing the bottle on his thigh.

"Thank you." That was the first time anyone had actually done something in regards to my dreams. Something to maybe help me make sense of it all.

"The DNA could be anyone. Could be the ex-boyfriend, although he won't provide a sample to clear himself. But it wouldn't be a red flag if it was on there. She did live with him."

Made sense. So basically, we were still in the same exact spot as we started. *With nothing.*

Jace pointed to the tv. "Good movie."

"I know right?" I stretched out my legs along the couch. "I loved Robin Williams."

"I'm a Mrs. Doubtfire man myself."

"Stop." I laughed.

"It's true." He chuckled.

"I can't believe we actually agreed on something."

"Don't get your hopes up. I'm not usually this amicable."

"Believe me, I don't have high hopes for you, Jace Foster." I crossed my ankles. "You've remained the same hard ass since the day I met you."

His eyes flickered. My comment was just a tease, but it was almost as if he was offended.

"Just part of the job." His eyes moved up my legs, then to my face.

"So, you keep saying." I angled my head, trying to get a read on him.

"Your feet, are they better?" He asked.

"They're fine." I shrugged and pulled my knees up to my chest.

He sat his beer to the side and stood. I followed his movement across the living room until he stopped at the end of the couch and sat down.

"Let me see." He motioned his hand.

I rolled my eyes. "I told you they are fine.

"Give me your foot, Sunshine."

I hated when he called me that. Mostly because it melted off another icy layer that I have placed around my heart.

Narrowing my eyes, I stretched my leg out, placing my foot in his hand. He tilted it, running his finger along my heel where the glass had cut me. They still had a pink tinge, but were mostly healed.

He frowns. Then moves his fingers up over my ankle bone. "I didn't see this last time."

I glanced down. A blue bruise had formed down the side of my ankle.

His finger lightly traced it. "You may have sprained it. Did you ice it?"

I laughed lightly at his sudden concern. "I think I'll be ok doc. You could always just kiss and make it better," I joked.

His hand gripped the arch of my foot, and he peered up at me over his lashes that I've recently become insanely jealous of. I would kill for that volume. He blinked, before moving his gaze back down to the bruise on my ankle. With one hand wrapped around the arch of my foot, the other slid just beneath my calf, raising my leg. I watched in awe as he lowered his head and placed the most delicate kiss I've ever received over my skin. It was a joke. A flirty comment I was sure he would brush off, or even completely ignore. It never even occurred to me he would comply. The warmth of his lips set a fire blazing all over my body. I didn't move as he leaned back up to meet my eyes. Like aways, his emotions weren't blasted across his face. He appeared calm. The only give away was the squeeze he gave my foot before his thumb pressed into my arch, trailing all the way down to my heel.

"Better?" He lifted a brow, but kept his posture relaxed.

I nodded. I was anything but. I was petrified to move. If I did I was most likely going to do something improper like climb across the length of this couch and straddle his lap. *That's definitely out of the question.* So, I stared motionless as he continued to massage my foot, never breaking his eyes from mine.

The heat began to travel down my neck, across my breasts, and down my stomach. We were venturing into dangerous territory and I knew I needed to stop this before it went any further.

"I should probably go to bed," I said through a deep breath.

He studied me for a moment, before he pressed his thumb back into the center of my arch. "That's probably a good idea."

Then why weren't either of us making an attempt to leave? To stop whatever the hell was happening? The silence stretched. The fire crackled in the background, but it was nothing compared to the sound of whatever fire that just ignited between us. I opened my mouth to speak, just as his phone rang. He still didn't move. It rang again.

"You should get that." I swallowed as I pulled my foot away from his grip.

He hesitated, before he dug into his pocket as I stood from the couch. When I peered over I saw it was my father.

Jace cleared his throat and swiped the screen. "Hey Cap."

He listened for a moment then his eyes flickered up to mine. "No. She's asleep. I'm not with her."

And that's exactly what I needed. A reminder.

CHAPTER 28

Jace

I went into the precinct today to pull all the information we had on the missing women Camille had in the cellar. It wasn't that I believed her, or that I didn't, I just needed to see for myself. Put together my own opinion. From just a glance it didn't appear these cases were related. The first girl was troubled. She had ran away from home more than once and was marked as a runaway. The second was similar. According to the mother she got hooked up with the wrong crowd and they were trying to convince her to leave Colorado and head East. It seemed each woman had either a record, or were in a rough spot. I saw how it could easily be considered a life choice situation and they moved on to more serious matters. But in the back of my mind, something wasn't sitting right. This was a small town. Three "runaways" in a matter of a few years is concerning. I know things run differently here. The man power is different and sometimes being on the inside can cloud your vision. Blur the facts.

I started to look at it as if it was a serial case. We had solved more than one back in Mississippi. I had to go back to the basics, and start from scratch. I had the day to myself since Camille was with Elle. It was Elle's birthday and I somehow got dragged into attending the party tonight at The Peak. Something was in the air. Maybe it was the new chill from the snow, or the fact I felt our dynamic shift last night. All I know is I'm on edge. Anxious. And one wrong move could put me in a deep pile of shit.

I showed up at the bar around 8:00. Adam, Rex, Easton, and Hank were already in the middle of a pool game.

"Jace." Easton nodded to me and I held up a hand, motioning to the bar.

The bartender handed me a beer before I made my way over to the pool table. It was a busy night and the band wasn't bad. I needed to kick back. I've felt wound tight for weeks. I couldn't help but scan the room. I was searching for blonde hair and a pair of legs that could make any grown man cry. But I came up empty. She wasn't here yet.

"How's it going Jace?" Hank waddled around the table and stuck out his hand.

I shook it with a firm grip. "Pretty good."

"We were just discussing the big event," Rex says as he chalks his pool stick.

"The big event?" I ask.

"June is turning four in February." Easton smiled.

Easton is a badass. He's a damn good cop and he still makes his little girl a priority. I salute him. I wouldn't be equipped to handle a kid on my own. Hell, I can't even handle a normal relationship.

"We've narrowed it down to Princess, My Little Pony, or Frozen." Rex sank a solid. "I'm rooting for Frozen. That Olaf is fucking hilarious."

"Frozen is my vote too." Easton downs the rest of his beer. "We already have the costume."

"What the hell is Frozen?" I ask as I lean back against a bar top table.

All four of them whip their heads in my direction. Astonishment written on their faces.

"That's it. This requires an intervention," Rex declares.

I chuckle and my eyes pull towards the door. Like I knew she was walking through at that exact moment. *Sunshine.* She shakes the loose snow from her hair and shrugs off her coat. A cream sweater is tucked into her jeans that reveal entirely too much for my liking. Because if I notice, so do the other men in here tonight. Elle steps in behind her, flanked by Bekka and Tilly, then the face that follows makes my fist clench. *Dustin.*

Elle is wearing a pink birthday crown, complete with a pink sash that says *birthday babe.* She latches onto Camille's arm as they slink their way through the crowd to the bar. Dustin trails behind them and I already feel it in my bones that tonight isn't going to go as planned. I can't relax with that asshole following Camille like a lost puppy.

"You want in on the next game?" Adam asks.

I tear my eyes away from her. "Count me in."

I distracted myself with the game. Long enough to let the girls get a couple of drinks and then make their rounds before they came over to the pool table. Bekka went straight over to Adam and Elle flung herself into Hank's arms. Camille's eyes flickered to mine before she let Rex wrap her up in a hug.

"I think we owe the birthday girl a round of shots!" Hank drops an arm over Elle's shoulder with a grin.

"I agree." Adam kissed the side of Bekka's head. "They're on you."

Tilly bounced on her heels and her hands flew up so fast I couldn't register what she said even if I tried, then she headed to the bar.

"Happy Birthday Ellie," Easton said in a hushed tone that I concluded was meant for only her to hear.

She rolls her lips together and nods. "Thanks East."

Her smile is there, but it's lacking, like it almost hurts. Oddly his looks the same and I make note of how he tracks every move when she walks over to another table of locals. There's a mixture of emotion in his eyes. Longing. Pain. Regret. He finally drops his gaze back to the game like he didn't just lay out all his cards with one look.

"Jace, you're up," he says as he reaches for his beer.

I stand and pick up my pool stick, then round the table to get a better shot. At least that's the story I'm sticking with. It's not the fact Camille is on that same side, watching me intently. I haven't seen her all day and the fact I'm using a lame ass excuse like a pool game to get closer to her is fucking ridiculous.

She stepped back so I could get in position. I leaned down, aiming in just the right spot before I tapped the ball, sending it into the corner pocket.

"Impressive, detective," she mused.

I kept my face flat as I backed up, settling next to her while Rex went to take his shot.

"How was your day, Sunshine?" I kept my eyes on the green felt.

A light chuckle left her before she nudged me with her elbow. "We're in public, Jace. We don't want people thinking we're actually friends."

In true Camille fashion, she strutted across to Tilly who had a tray full of shots balancing on her shoulder and sang out the entire Happy Birthday song to Elle. Solo.

Chapter 29

Camille

Jace looked down right edible tonight. Which was not helping my desire to hate him. And it wasn't helping that two women just sauntered over to him and another friend of Adam's that showed up with that gleam in their eyes. I tried to ignore it. I tried to focus on dancing with Elle and listening to Bekka and Tilly talk about the station gossip. But the closer the tall red head with the gigantic breasts got to Jace, the more uncomfortable I felt.

A soft touch landed on the small of my back. Dustin smiled, showing off his straight white teeth and boyish features. "Need a drink, Cami?"

I caught a glimpse of Jace when I turned to answer him. I had planned to say no, but when the woman leaned in to whisper in his ear, and he laughed, my stomach almost fell to the first floor.

I moved my attention to Dustin. "I'd love one."

He winked before he flagged down Kyle. My own hands slid up and down my arms, like I was trying to sooth myself. Trying to rid myself of this nagging feeling settling inside me. *I didn't like it. At all.* Elle giggled next to me as Bekka pointed to a man across the bar. Elle had already made a point to tell me she was getting lucky tonight. She's just trolling for her best option. The next man she thinks will make her forget.

"I'll be back." She shimmied her shoulders. "Or maybe I won't." She made her way over to the man nestled in the corner of the room, alone.

She wasn't four steps away from me when I saw Easton perched against the far wall. He watched her glide across the floor and to my surprise, he sat down his beer and he met her in the middle of the dance floor before she could get to the stranger. He said something in her ear and when she started to protest, he just gently tugged on her elbow until she was close enough for him to pull her in for a dance.

"Here you go, Cam." Dustin handed me my drink and I thanked him with a smile.

He wasn't a terrible guy. A player yes, but he was nice enough. Maybe he would be nice enough to get my mind off the asshole detective canoodling in the corner. Elle said it herself. I need to make sure my needs as a woman are met. Then maybe I will be less likely to something completely irrational like get jealous over Jace freaking Foster. *Now I'm annoyed.*

"I need the ladies' room," I told Dustin before I weaved through the crowd to the back of the bar.

It was finally quiet, but I could still hear the clouded sounds of conversation and music. I had just sat down on the toilet when the door opened.

"Girl. He's so into you," a woman said.

"He's so fucking hot," she admitted.

"So is the other one. And he's a firefighter," the other gushes.

I still, clenching the waist band of my jeans.

"Jace said he's staying at a cabin not far from here. Sounds like an invitation to me."

Jace. He's taking her home. To *my* home.

Nausea. A hefty wave of it filtered through me at the thought of him and *her.* In my house. Across the hall.

"The night is young," the other chirps.

The sink water that was running turns off, then the door opens and it's quiet again. Too quiet. My thoughts are way too loud. My feelings way too *hurt.*

"Get it together, Camille," I murmur to myself after I step out of the stall and approach the mirror.

Dustin. Yes. I have *Dustin.*

After I've regained enough composure, I straighten my sweater, run my hands through my hair, then walk out into the hall. I had only gotten two steps in when Tilly appeared in front of me.

"What's wrong?" She asked.

"Nothing." I shook my head.

She lifts a blonde eyebrow. "You're lying. I know you."

I pick a piece of imaginary fuzz from my sleeve. "I'm fine."

She crosses her arms. "You're my twin, Cami. You think I can't feel when something is wrong?" She pauses. "You think I don't feel when you *feel?*"

The look on her face makes my heart sink. It's a blessing and a curse. I hate that she feels when something is hurting me. Unfortunately, I feel when others hurt, so it's a circle of misery. I glance over her shoulder and see the same girl slide up next to Jace.

"It's him, isn't it?" She asks.

It's only us in the corner, so she's talking. I wish she would do it more often. She has no clue how proud I am of her.

"Who?" I ask like I'm completely clueless.

"Detective dick," she mocks.

I snort out a laugh and she wraps her arm around my shoulder, leaning her head against mine. "He likes you."

"He does not," I deadpan.

"Whatever you say Cam," she singsongs.

"I'll see you later. Behave." I point a stern finger at her, but she just waved me off with a laugh.

I immediately found Dustin who was talking with Rex and a man I didn't recognize.

"Hey, you mind taking me home?" I asked him.

He frowned. "You already done for the night?"

Rex gave me a curious look, so I leaned in closer to whisper in Dustin's ear. "I just need to get a few things. I was hoping...maybe we could go to your place?"

He grins and his hand slides to my waist. "You bet."

"Let me just say bye to Elle." I gave his arm a squeeze as I searched the room.

She was nowhere to be seen. I quickly said goodnight to Bekka who looked baffled when I told her I was leaving with Dustin. She knows the tension that's been between me and Jace. I may have slipped a little during our brunch this morning and shared the unexpected events of last night. It's starting to screw with my mind.

"I'm ready," I announced.

Dustin beamed before we grabbed our coats from the rack. I took one more look over my shoulder. I couldn't help it. I wish I would have been stronger. Because when the woman wrapped her arms around Jace's neck and brought her lips to his I almost stopped breathing all together. I turned away and quickly trotted down the stairs. No use in torturing myself. No use in upsetting myself over a man who sees me as nothing but an obligation.

CHAPTER 30

Jace

Kelly, or was it Kendall? I can't remember, wraps her around my neck. She leans in, closing her eyes. I'm assuming she's waiting for me to meet her half way, but I'm not focused on her. I'm focused on the empty spot across the room where Camille just stood. My hands reach up, slightly tugging on her wrists to remove her arms.

"Sorry Kelly. It's not gonna happen," I rasp out.

"It's Brittany." She pouts.

Well then, I was way off.

"Brittany." I correct. "Sorry. Gotta go."

I slip by her as she mutters "asshole" under her breath.

I don't see Camille. I study the room quickly, then spot Rex close to the exit. "Hey." I nod. "You see Camille come through here?"

He lifts a brow and crosses his bulky arms. "Yeah, she just left a couple of minutes ago with Dustin."

"Dustin? West?" I question.

"Yep. Thought it was weird considering you two have been eye fucking each other all night." He motions to me and then downstairs.

"I wasn't eye.." I start.

"Foster. Cut the shit. Go get her before she ends up with the panty crickets."

"Panty crickets?" I shake my head. "Never mind."

I jogged down stairs, scooting through the restaurant area before I made it outside. It was cold tonight and the snow was getting heavier by the hour. I peered down to my right. The sidewalk was empty, then I peered to my left over a group of teenagers and saw Camille huddled by the edge of the building. *No Dustin.*

I tugged my coat around me before I started towards her.

"Where's Dustin?" It came out harsh. Half way angry, which I was.

I didn't want to admit it, but I was jealous. *So, fucking jealous.*

She startled, shoving her hands into her coat pockets. "He's getting the truck." She glanced behind me as if looking for someone.

"Why are you out here in the cold?" I asked.

"Why do you care?" She glared at me before giving me her back.

"What the fuck are you doing leaving with West?" I scoffed.

"Again, not sure why you care."

I stepped towards her. "You're not leaving with him."

She laughed out loud and pulled her hands from her coat, lifting her fingers up to run them through her hair. "So, what are you now, Jace? My daddy?"

I refuse to even admit the impure thoughts that just skated through my mind at that question. The answer on the tip of my tongue wasn't much better.

"I'm relieving you. You have the night off." She waves a hand at the building. "Go get your world rocked by some bar fly."

"What bar fly are you referring to?" I cocked my head to the side.

She rolled her eyes in aggravation. "The woman you've been fumbling with all night!"

"Fumbling?" I quirk a brow.

"You know what I mean," she hisses. "I'm leaving so you can do whatever you want. I'm sure it's not been easy with me in the house. I know you men have certain needs...and you've made it clear all you need is a warm body."

She thinks I'm taking Kelly home. *Katy. Brittany. Shit.*

"That's why you're leaving with him?"

"Maybe I need my world rocked too," she sasses back.

Over my dead body.

"Look, Jace it's none of my business what you do off the clock."

"You seem to be making it your business." I smirked. "You sure are going out of your way to accommodate me."

"I'm your host remember?" She gave me her back again as she faced the street. "It's my job."

She threw my words right back in my face. The words I had been telling her since day one. Although, me arguing with her in the freezing cold about who she's allowed to sleep with is a far cry from my *job.*

"Camille, just go home." I sighed.

"Go home?" She whirled around. "Why on earth would I go home right now? To listen to you fuck some other woman in *my* house."

She pointed at her chest. "God, it literally makes sick. Physically ill to think of you in bed with her." She shakes her head. "You know what, I can't do this."

"Camille." My hands that are resting in my pocket slide out.

She shakes her head. "No. You just go. Please. I don't want to feel like this. I don't even know what this is. I hate it." She turns to the street again, before turning back to me. "It's dumb right?" She laughs and it's bordering a sob.

"Stop talking." My steps are heavy as I lift my boots from the snow. I stalk towards her until she backs up, into the alley way.

"You don't even like me," she continues. "Maybe you just need to move out. I promise I won't do anything stupid. I think we need space."

"Stop. Fucking. Talking," I bark out just as her back hits the wall and I close the space, pressing my forehead to hers. "Please," I whisper.

She sucks in a breath. *It makes me physically ill.* I know exactly what she's feeling. My hands flex as I brace them on the wall above her head. My heart slams against my rib cage and I keep telling myself to step back. To walk away before I do something really fucking stupid on a public street.

A car horn honks, shaking us loose from the moment and I make the smartest decision I've made all night. I step away from her.

The truck window rolls down. "Camille!"

She turns to look at Dustin, then back at me. She hasn't moved yet and part of me wishes she wouldn't. The other part is praying she does. Her brows pinch, like she's analyzing the pros and cons. Stand here with me, or go with him. Either one is likely to get her into trouble.

"I'll see you later," she says before she pushes off the wall and starts towards his truck.

I should let her leave. I should let him take her home. I should walk back in and take whatever her name is to the nearest hotel. But if I do that, if I let her leave with him...my eyes close and my hands are back against the brick. I picture him touching her.....kissing her.

Fuck that.

My palms forcefully leave the wall, and all too quickly I'm storming towards Camille's back. Just as she climbs in the passenger seat and pulls the door shut, my hand catches the handle. Her eyes widen when I yank it open.

"Get out," I say.

"What?" She gasps.

"I said get out of the truck," I repeat.

"What the hell is your problem, Foster?" Dustin leans over the steering wheel to see around Camille.

"West, this doesn't concern you." I keep my eyes on hers. "I'm only gonna tell you one more time, Sunshine. Get your ass out of the truck."

Her fingers grip the leather, anchoring herself to the seat with defiance written all over her pretty face. Dustin mutters something about me losing my mind, but I'm still focused on her as she actively shoots daggers at me. She hasn't budged an inch, so like a man of my word, I don't say it again. I shove my arms forward, scooping her out of the seat in one swift move.

"What the fu.."

I don't hear the rest of Dustin's rant because I've already slammed the door and I'm in route to my truck just behind the sidewalk.

"You are freaking insane! You know that?!!" She shouts. Her face is contorted, angry even, but she's not kicking or fighting to get out of my grip.

I reach my truck, and pull open the door, depositing her in my front seat. "Don't move."

She huffs and crosses her arms as I round the hood of the car. When I jump in, she turns to face me, her mouth ready to tell me exactly what kind of asshole I am. *Preaching to the choir, baby.*

I decided in that moment I was done. Done with the run around. Done with avoiding whatever the hell's been hanging between us. Her cheeks were flushed, her hair slightly disheveled, and I wanted nothing more than to tear those fucking jeans right off her body. But there was time for that later, right now I just needed this. I reached across the console. My palm gripped the nape of her neck. I tugged hard enough she sprang forward and without another thought to the consequences, or why this was a really bad idea, I kissed her.

CHAPTER 31

Camille

It might have been an earthquake. Or an avalanche that tumbled down the nearest mountain. Something happened in the atmosphere that vibrated every single part of my existence. When his mouth met mine, I was in complete shock. *Was I hallucinating?* But when I felt his tongue flick against my lip, requesting passage, I melted. I melted into his kiss, his touch, everything that went against every fiber of my being. I broke the kiss with a gasp. I was almost in his lap. One knee was balanced on the console and one of my hands on the steering wheel.

His thumb traced my lower lip. "This is your chance." His voice was low and it ricocheted through me. "If you don't want this you need to tell me now."

"What is.... this?" I swallowed.

His thumb made another trail across my lip and he smirked. It was arrogant, like he knew he had me right where he wanted me. I tried to squeeze my thighs together. My position made it impossible, so I had to embrace the undying throb that began between my legs. I didn't want it, then again I welcomed it. It was a mixture of lust and frustration and I would bet the farm he felt the same.

"When we get home. I'm taking every single piece of clothing off of you." He leaned in, placing a kiss right under my ear and I shuttered.

"So..." he whispered. "Speak now, Sunshine."

Speak? I was barely breathing.

I nodded. "Ok."

This man just said he wanted to take off my clothes and all I could think to say was "ok."

Real lame, Camille

"Ok?" He asked with one more kiss that made me squirm against the leather.

"Ok."

He pulled away and smiled. Then his hand reached back, slapping me on the ass. "Buckle up."

The twenty-minute drive home was excruciating. I couldn't sit still. Jace's hand rested on my thigh, running circles with his fingertips like that was gonna help. All it did was make it worse and the amount of moisture pooling in my underwear right now was plain embarrassing. I kept sneaking glimpses of him out of the corner of my eye. He was relaxed, one arm hung over the steering wheel and the other on me. I haven't seen him like this. He's always so guarded. Stoic. *Grumpy.*

When we pulled up to the house, I was reminded why I loved this time of year. Snow blanketed the yard and the paths leading down to the lake. It was beautiful. During my observations, Jace had come around the hood and opened my door. I hopped down, fishing around in my purse for my keys before I let us into the warmth of the cabin.

Achilles came trotting around the couch with a yawn. I scratched his ear when he approached, cooing words to him only dog moms understand.

"Outside, "Jace said as he held open the door for him.

I watched him let Achilles out and lock the door. It hit me how we've fell into a routine. Even though there was obvious tension, we've learned to co-exist. I sat my bag on the counter and that's when I felt him. The weight of his chest pressed against my back. His palms came up, running up the length of my arms, to my shoulders, where he spun me to face him.

With his blue eyes never wavering from mine, his fingers inched down my sides, bunching up the fabric of my shirt until it came untucked from my jeans. I lifted my arms, giving him permission to remove it. The cream sweater landed just behind me on the floor, then his hands were back on me. I took in his hungry gaze. It was fixated on the black lace bra I was still wearing.

"Is this ok?" He asked.

His voice was soft. Gentle. He was a completely different man right now. Attentive. I wondered what triggered the change. Maybe he was just smooth when he had his sights set on something. Maybe he was good at turning up the charm to get what he wanted. None of that really mattered right now. I'd sell my left kidney just to have his hands on me all night.

He shocked me by lowering to his knees. The hardwood creaked beneath his weight as he landed soft kisses across my abdomen. Tingles shot through every cell in my body, and my fingers dove into his dark hair. It was thick and I ran my fingers through it, coaxing him to keep going.

His lips reached the waist band of my jeans, so I moved my hands to the button, but he swatted them away.

"I told you *I* was taking every piece of clothing off of you." He flickered his eyes up to me and I grinned at his attempt to scold me.

"I apologize," I quipped.

His large hands slowly peeled off my jeans. It was painfully erotic. I wanted him to hurry, but I wanted to savor every second at the same time. I peered down at Jace, on his knees in my kitchen. I giggled.

"Something funny, Sunshine?" He asked, tossing my jeans behind me as well.

I shook my head. "Just never pictured you as the kind of man who got on his knees."

He chuckled as he fervently watched his hands trail up my legs, squeezing my outer thighs when he reached them. "The pain is worth it."

I lifted a brow. "You're in pain?"

He laughed low again and placed a soft kiss right at my hip bone. "I'm trying really hard to take this slow."

"Why slow?" I reached a hand out, running it through his hair as he traveled to my other hip.

"I plan to take my time. Remember every part of you," he whispered.

I knew what he was saying. *Because this would never happen again.*

"Because this is a one-night thing?" I breathed out.

His lips froze against me. He dropped his head, leaning his forehead against my stomach. "Camille...you know.."

"I know," I interrupted.

I know he was going against the rules right now. Against my father. I know he doesn't do more than one night. And soon he would be back in the city. Back to his life.

"I need to follow the captain's orders." He looked up at me. "I need to get released to field duty. I need those release papers. I need control back, Camille."

His hands glided around my waist. "I *need* to be focused."

"I understand," I whispered.

His gaze moved to my lips as he stood to his feet. "As much as I need those things." His own lips feathered across my cheek, down the side of my neck, then back up, hovering only millimeters away from mine. "I *need* this more."

My hands ran over the curve of his shoulders, down his arms to intertwine his fingers with mine. "Then take me upstairs."

CHAPTER 32

Jace

With her consent, I dipped down, so I could sling her over my shoulder. This time her bare ass was right against my chin. She shrieked when I started up the stairs and I let my hand drift back to pull up the fabric of her thong, snapping it against her flesh. That earned me another squeal and I paused when I got to the top.

"Your room or mine?" I asked over my shoulder.

"Mine," she called out.

I stepped across the hall and as soon as I was close enough to the bed, I laid her back against it.

"No angry tossing this time?" She smiled as she leaned up on her elbows.

I reached for her ankle, jerking her down to the edge of the bed. She was so beautiful. Soft skin and curves I doubt I would ever find again.

The black lace was such a contrast to her light skin and I couldn't keep my hands from exploring every exposed inch. My fingers hooked on the sides of her thong, then I paused.

"I thought you didn't wear underwear."

She slightly bit her lip and smiled. "I just said that to get a rise out of you."

"You got one. I nearly choked to death." I slid them down her legs and tossed them aside. "Take off your bra," I instructed as my hands ran up the inside of her thighs.

"I thought *you* were taking off my clothes."

"Are you always this insubordinate?" I nudged her legs open as I lowered down to the floor.

"It's an ongoing issue." She peered down at me with amused eyes.

"I guess we need to fix that, don't we?"

I was done talking. This was probably the most fluent conversation we've had, but I had other things in mind.

"I mean I don't see an issue wi...." she started.

"Sunshine," I warned.

She silenced.

"Stop talking." My tone was enough for her to snap her mouth shut.

I leaned down, dropping a kiss on the inside of her thigh before I spread her legs even farther apart, barring every intimate part of herself to me. She didn't shy away, she let her legs fall back as she reached behind her back, unsnapping her bra. She slowly slipped it off of her shoulders, never breaking eye contact as she dropped it next to the bed.

"Fuck," I murmured.

I could feel my cock pressing against my jeans. It was borderline painful, but this wasn't about me right now, this was about her. I wanted her to come apart. *For me.* Not Dustin fucking West, or that douche bag ex of hers. *Me.* Her hips shifted as she squirmed against the sheets. She was impatient, and quite frankly I was tired of pretending that I knew this wasn't going to happen. I'm pretty positive I knew the moment I saw her in that kitchen we would eventually end up here.

I lowered my head down, closing my eyes as I listened to the sounds she made. The heaviness of her breath and the soft frustrated growl that left her lips when I hovered over the spot that I expected to devour within the next five seconds.

"Jace..." she moaned.

And that was all the encouragement I needed.

With one slow stroke of my tongue, she was arching her back. "Oh my God.."

I smiled against her and repeated the motion, hoping to pull the same reaction, in which she granted me another string of words laced with a moan. She was vocal, and I had zero complaints. I already knew she was a talker; I just didn't know it would carry over into the bedroom. Apparently, it does. My hands flattened against her thighs, pinning them to the mattress as I continued my assault, pulling cries and encouragements from her lips. Every part of her was enthralling. Her voice, her mind, her body. *Her taste.* She was like clay in my hands and I molded her into the perfect work of art when she finally screamed my name. And fell apart. *For me.*

I felt her release as it coated my tongue and my ears have never heard anything as soul moving as when my name repeatedly tumbled from her mouth. I know I said one night. I know it should never happen again. It's against the rules.

But, at this point. It's inevitable.

CHAPTER 33

Camille

I couldn't move even if I tried. I was shaken. *Literally.* It took me a second to catch my breath and let my vision clear up. I've never in my life had an orgasm that intense.

My head tilted as I sluggishly pushed up on my elbows to look at the man responsible for the epic turn of events. He wore that arrogant grin, only this time, it was definitely warranted.

"That was..." I almost snorted a laugh, but I cleared my throat. "I've never..."

He stood and his hand went to the back of his neck, where he ripped his shirt over his head. That one move in itself may have been hotter than the look he gave me from between my legs moments ago.

"You've never what?"

Embarrassment eased into me as I faltered my words. "No one has ever.....been...done that," I finally got out.

His hands froze on the button of his jeans. "He never did that for you?"

I knew the *he,* he was referring to was Stuart. I shook my head no.

"I knew he was a fucking douche," he muttered as he unzipped his jeans. "I'm assuming he never made you come either?"

My silence was answer enough for him. He shoved his jeans down his thighs and stepped out, presenting himself in nothing but a pair of grey boxer briefs that allowed me to see all of him. *Every inch.*

Detective *dick* was in no way lacking.

The briefs went next, and *oh shit.* I swallowed down the words as I watched his cock reveal itself from the material. I was momentarily mesmerized. I don't think I've ever had the thought, *that's a pretty dick,* but I guess there's a first time for everything. His hand moved, fisting himself as he spoke to me. I couldn't relay a word he said because I was caught up in the motion of his hand, making lazy strokes, *up and down.*

"Camille."

"Mmhm," I hummed, still not moving my eyes from the show.

"Look at me," he said.

"I am," I whispered.

"I want your eyes on mine."

I slowly dragged my gaze up his torso, across his chest, then up to his eyes.

"Did you hear me?" He asked. His hand dropped and he let one of his knees dip onto the mattress in front of me.

"I was a bit.... Distracted," I admitted.

He lifted an eyebrow. "Well, now that I have your attention." He slowly crawled, positioning his naked body over mine. "I can promise you." He leaned down, placing a warm kiss on the top of my breast. "When you're with me." Another kiss was placed on the column of my throat. "I will make you come. Every. Single. Time."

I'm officially ruined.

I had a feeling Jace Foster wasn't the kind of man that didn't make good on his promises and I was giddy over the fact I would be on the receiving end. His hand cupped my breast, then he slid it down my stomach, until he reached between my legs. Two fingers glided into my opening and I tilted my head back, welcoming the pressure. His eyes veered over to my night stand and I tensed.

"I don't have any condoms," I whispered.

Disappointment imbedded in my stomach when he slid his hand away. *Well, that was fun while it lasted.*

"Do you?" I asked.

"I have one in my wallet," he answered, but he didn't move.

I'm not sure the exact moment this all derailed, but my heart sank. *Why is he stopping?* Maybe his mind cleared. Maybe he's realizing this is reckless and he's coming to his senses.

His eyes found mine, and like he could read the insecurity racing across my face, he leaned in, placing a gentle kiss on my lips. "I want to feel you."

His tip nudged my entrance and it registered what he meant. Our eyes locked and I could see the question being relayed without even a word. *Do you trust me?*

Did I trust him? I answered my own question when I lifted my legs, wrapping them around his waist, giving him enough pressure to signal what I wanted. *I want to feel all of him.*

With my silent consent, his hips thrusted forward. He entered me with ease, sending tingles dancing up my spine. His grip left my hips, then he caught my hands, lacing our fingers as he lifted them over my head, bracing them against the pillow.

He plunged into me, deeper and deeper until our flesh connected. The pain of him stretching me was mixed with pleasure as he began to move with purpose. His forehead rested against mine, and I cried out when his next thrust already had me on the verge of tipping over the edge. Everything inside of me ignited. All of the feelings I had been fighting. It was almost overwhelming. It wasn't just the physical. It wasn't just the fact I was on the brink of another catastrophic orgasm. It was *him.* This exploding sense of connection in my chest as he looked into my eyes. He could feel it. I know he could, but I doubt he would ever admit it.

His breathe was hot and heavy, matching the air that surrounded us. His lips scraped across my temple, then landed on my ear. "Are you gonna come for me, baby?"

Yes. Yes I am.

My thighs flexed around his waist and he unlatched his hands from mine. With a one swipe, the pillow was jerked out from under my head, and placed underneath my hips, which he lifted with one arm. The angle was new, and when sank down inside of me even further, I unraveled.

"Jace.." I wasn't sure why I was saying his name. It was a warning, a praise, or maybe I just needed to remind myself this was actually happening.

"Fuck..." he gritted out. Followed by another ragged, "Fuck, fuck, fuck."

That was it. One more thrust.

The scream that left my throat was piercing as light burst from every corner of the room. Or so it felt. I felt the orgasm straight down to my toes and it peaked just as he swelled inside of me. His warmth filled me and with his head bowed to my chest, he emptied himself inside me.

When the fog cleared and we both relaxed into each other, the consequences of what we had just done reared its ugly head.

Because I knew in that exact moment I didn't just give Jace Foster my body, I gave him my heart.

And I would never recover when he gave it back.

CHAPTER 34

Camille

I have never slept so hard. When my eyes blinked open this morning, my body was strangely relaxed. Our *one night* lasted until the early hours of this morning and I could tell by the position of the sun I had slept past my alarm.

Although I was rested, I had a heavy weight drop on me when I rolled over to an empty bed. I expected it. I knew it would be empty. But I didn't think it would feel like this. My hand landed against the cold sheets that housed his body a few hours ago and I closed my eyes. It was still fresh. Still vivid in my mind. I could almost feel the brush of his lips against my skin. I let out a deep breath, popping open my eyes. *Get up.* There's a woman to find and work to be done. I didn't have time to dwell on Jace Foster. He was out of reach. Physically and emotionally. It was best to push last night to the back of my memories and move on.

With a new determination, I rolled over, landed on my feet, and hit the ground running. My three empty cabins needed to be cleaned and revamped for the Christmas holiday. Mr. Sumner still occupied cabin one for five more days, so his would have to wait.

It took all day, but three of my cabins were now ready to welcome my Christmas guests that were arriving this coming weekend. I checked my phone as I drove back up to the main house. I told myself I wasn't checking to see if Jace called, or texted, but I was. Not one word.

It was 7:00 now, and I had just walked through my front door when my phone buzzed. It wasn't Jace, it was Adam.

Adam: We need you at the station.

I was ready in record time, and drove at a frantic speed to the station. My stomach was in knots about what could be wrong. Maybe they found her. Maybe they found *him*.

It was almost eight by the time I pushed through the glass doors of the squad room. My eyes darted around the room, and landed on my father who spoke with Hollis on the far side by the map of Timber Creek that was tacked against the wall.

"Camille," Adam called my name and I turned to see him coming towards me, followed by Jace.

We briefly made eye contact before I gave my attention to Adam. "What's wrong?"

"A girl came in. She has something to report and she will only speak to you."

"Me?" I glanced around him.

"She's in room one." He motioned.

"Alone?" I asked.

"Yeah, she came in alone."

I nodded and followed him down the hallway. Jace was behind me and even with the high anticipation of who sat behind this door, I felt the air thick between us.

Adam stepped in first and on the couch sat a girl no more than nineteen. Blonde hair with sunken eyes. She tugged her coat tighter as I stepped through. I gave her a smile to hopefully calm her nerves. I glanced back at Adam, giving him a nod. He closed the door, and it was just us girls left in the room.

"Hi, I'm Camille." I sat my purse on the table and took a seat at the opposite end of the couch.

"I'm Laramie." She spoke softly, avoiding eye contact and began fidgeting with her hands.

"Adam, the man who brought you in here is my brother. He said you wanted to talk to me," I offered.

Her boots were worn and her jeans ripped. I wasn't sure if it was by style choice, or inability to buy new ones. She seemed nervous.

"My sister goes to the Timber Creek Center." She turned and faced me. "Tilly is her teacher. She's your sister right?"

"Yes. She's my twin." I smiled.

"My sister says she trusts Tilly, and I trust her, so I guess since you're her sister, I can trust you."

"Of course, you can trust me. Can I ask what this is about?" I folded my hands in my lap.

"Six months ago, a man attempted to kidnap me at Piney State Park."

Every hair on my neck stood up.

"I was able to get away, but I never reported it. My choices wouldn't be exactly...seen as acceptable, so I didn't think anyone would believe someone like me."

"Choices?" I asked.

She lowered her head in shame.

"Can I ask why you were at the park?"

"I was there to meet someone. To meet this man." She watched my reaction and I did my best not to show judgment as she continued. "I met him on PictureMe App."

"What is that? I'm not familiar."

"It's like an OnlyFans...." she trailed off.

She was selling.... herself.

"I know what you're thinking," she blurted.

I held up a hand to stop her, then gently rested it on her arm. "What I'm thinking is you're a victim. Someone tried to hurt you, but you got away. It doesn't matter the circumstances."

She nodded as tears filled her eyes. "I don't typically meet men, but we had been talking for a month or so and he seemed safe."

"I know what it's like to have to tell a story over and over. Especially when it's painful. Do you mind if I let my friend come in? He's a detective and he can write down everything you want us to know so we can find the man who did this."

She nodded. "That's fine." Her eyes glistened. "I think he got to Meredith."

Meredith.

I paused before I stood from the couch. "How do you know?"

"Because she was on the app too."

And just like that. There it is. The connection I had been looking for.

CHAPTER 35

Jace

I looked down at the notepad that held Laramie's statement. According-ing to her she agreed to meet the man on the outskirts of the park. That tells me he knew his way around. He knew what areas were regulated and where the check in locations were. She was consistent in her words. Never straying, or changing her story. They met and he immediately wanted to go on a walk. As soon as her back was turned, when they entered into the park, he was on her. She managed to hit him in the head with a rock and it gave her just enough time to get away.

"Can you describe him?" Camille asked.

"You know.... oddly, it was hard to see his face. He had a ball cap on. It was pulled really low and his coat collar was up." Her brows furrowed. "He's tall." She glanced over at me. "Not quite as tall you."

"Ok, so maybe six foot?" Camille asked.

"Yes." She shrugged. "I know it seems weird I can't describe him, but I really couldn't see all of him. Black coat. Green hat."

"Was he built? Muscular? Thin?"

"He wasn't muscular. He wasn't thin as a rail either. I would say average."

"Ok. That's good Laramie. Every little bit helps."

Laramie nodded. She's seemed more comfortable, not as anxious the longer Camille spoke to her. I watched closely. I had been a detective for years and seen some of the best female agents speak with witnesses or victims. None of them had an ounce of the compassion Camille did. It oozed out of her. *Kindness. Love. Acceptance.* She had a gift. She could make a brick wall talk back. Funny, how I was the one who could go weeks without talking to another human soul unless I had to, was paired with her.

"I think we can work with what you gave us. If I have any other questions is it ok if I call you?" Camille asked as they both stood.

"Yes that's fine." The girl slipped her small purse over her shoulder. "There is one more thing..." She gnawed at her lip with hesitation. "I don't know if it means anything or not." She faced Camille. "When he had me on the ground the only thing he said was 'I knew you'd be back, my golden angel.'"

Every ounce of blood drained from Camille's face, but she quickly recovered, blinking rapidly as she reached out, patting Laramie's arm. "Thank you Laramie. If you need anything at all, or if you ever feel unsafe. Please call me."

"Thank you, Camille." She looked over at me. "Thank you, detective."

I nodded back and followed them both into the hallway. No one would have noticed. No one here has been studying Camille Harper like I have these last few weeks. She was jarred. *Shaken.* And I needed to know why. Laramie left the building and I almost couldn't keep my hands off of Camille. I wanted to reach out, pull her into a private room and demand she tell me what that was. What she felt. But before I could, I heard her father call us over.

We crossed the crowded room, and into his office.

"How was the girl?" He asked.

"Scared," Camille said. She sighed and ran her hands through her hair. "A man tried to attack her outside Piney State Park six months ago."

He sat back in his chair, reaching his thumb and finger up to massage his temples. "Could she give us anything?"

"Enough. Met him on the PictureMe app. He's tall, average build. Black coat with a green hat," she said.

"I can get IT on the app. Try to pull what they can," I offered.

He nodded at me and sat up in his chair.

"So...it looks like I was on target. And I think we have more than enough reason to believe Meredith didn't leave town or just get lost in the mountain. Meredith was also on the app."

"Is this like a dating app?" Cap asked.

She glanced over at me.

"Not exactly. It's more of a.... way for some people to earn money," I said.

"Prostitution?" He gaped.

"No no. It's not that. It's mainly pictures and private conversations. It's all done via internet," Camille cut in.

"Regardless, this girl is a victim and Meredith could be too." He reached over, grabbing his phone. "Camille, thank you for helping with her. Can you give me a second with Foster?"

She ringed her hands together. "Of course," then she stepped out of the room, gaze glued to the linoleum as she passed me.

Captain made a quick call, muttering something into the phone before he hung up, giving me all of his attention.

"I need you to get with Adam tomorrow. It's late, but tomorrow I want to regroup. Now that we have this new information I want to look at this at a different angel."

"No problem. I'll get with him first thing in the morning."

"Good." He folded his hands together, propping them up on a folder. "I want to thank you for sticking with Camille. I know it wasn't ideal for you, I just...sometimes a father needs peace of mind so I can focus on what's in front of me. My job is important, but my kids always come first."

"It's not a problem." I shrugged. "I've always been good at my job, Cap. I take it seriously."

He nodded then met my eyes. "And I want to thank you for respecting my rules. Respecting my authority."

I froze. My throat thickening.

"I asked you to stay focused. Keep your job and her safety the priority. So far, I can see you've done that."

I've done a lot more than that.

"And," he continued. "I saw Dodge today. He said your house will be ready tomorrow. I'm sure you're ready to be back in your own space."

I dipped my head, my gut twisting inside out. Here he is giving me gratitude over a rule I threw right out the fucking window less than twenty-four hours ago.

"Thank you, sir." Was all I croaked out. There was a pause, a silence, and I felt the words slip out.

"Cap, we need to talk."

His eyes squinted and right when I started to confess, his door opened. "Richard. We need you in IT."

I clamped my mouth shut. Unsure of what the fuck I was about to do. All I knew was I wanted more than one night with her. I wanted a hell of a lot more.

"Foster, we'll talk in the morning."

He left the room and I ran a hand across my face. I had not one clue what I was doing anymore, but I knew exactly who I wanted to do it with. *Sunshine.* Which told me one thing. I was becoming attached. And that was a problem.

CHAPTER 36

Camille

I sat in my claw foot tub surrounded by bubbles and lavender scented candles. After the talk with Laramie, I needed to clear my mind. This was my way of reflecting. Refreshing my soul. When the bathroom door creaked opened, I rolled my head to the side to see Jace step in. His shirt was already unbuttoned, hanging open against his unbuttoned jeans.

Without a word he slipped off his shirt, then stepped out of his pants. My eyes wandered. I soaked in everything from his stubbled chin down to his feet. He was immaculate. Perfect shape. Perfect, *everything*. He stepped forward and casually threw one leg over the side of tub, joining me.

I scooted myself up, making room for his large size. "Exactly what do you think you are doing, detective?"

He lowered down into the water with a mischievous grin. "What's it look like I'm doing?"

"It looks like you are intruding."

He settled against the tub and cocked his head to the side. "You did good tonight."

"What do you mean? "I asked.

"With Laramie. You handled it well. She seemed comfortable with you."

I shrugged. "I just tried to be as authentic as I could. I treated her the same way I would want to be treated."

"I was impressed."

"Did you just compliment me, Jace Foster?" I teased.

With a deep rumble from his chest, his hands reached out underneath the soapy water, finding my legs. He ran his fingers up my calf, then proceeded the route to my thighs.

"What are you doing?" I whispered.

"Do you want me to leave?"

"You said one night." My voice was quiet.

The water was up to his chest, so I couldn't see his hands, but I felt them. I felt the trail of fire they left behind as they danced across my flesh. One finger glided between my legs and dipped inside me.

"I lied." A crooked smile came across his lips.

"And here I thought you were an honorable man." I let my legs fall open against each side of the tub.

He added another finger, sliding them in and out with slow precision. "I used to be." His eyes started to haze over with a familiar look I had come to recognize. "Until I met you."

"You're projecting." I smiled.

"Not projecting." He slipped his hand away. "Come here."

At first I stayed still. "Isn't this against the rules?"

"Yes."

"And the consequences?" I asked.

His hand found mine, and he brought it over to wrap around the base of his cock. "Does is feel like I give a damn about the consequences?"

I raised up on my knees, sloshing water over the edge of the full tub. Soapy suds drifted down my wet skin and his eyes moved right along with them. He leaned up just enough to tug me towards him, guiding me to straddle his lap. My breasts were only inches from his face, tempting him in the best possible way. He licked his lips before he brought my nipple into his mouth, sucking on the already sensitive bud.

My neck rolled back as he grazed his teeth across me, then moved to the next, repeating the same routine that I felt twinging in my core. I didn't even care that I told myself I should just move on. My hand found him again beneath the bubbles and with one shift of my hips, I was sinking down along his shaft. He groaned as I lifted up, and sank back down again. The groan was pleasure accompanied by a hint of frustration. Like he was angry with himself for giving in.

"You want to know the truth?" He said before his lips met mine. His tongue swirled, before he pulled back to look at me. "I told myself I wouldn't touch you again."

I rolled my hips. He closed his eyes and his hands slid around my waist, then down to grip my ass. "But then I saw you again today." His fingers kneaded into my skin. "I need one more time, Sunshine." He placed a kiss on my collar bone. "Last time."

I knew he was right. It had to be. This wasn't going to be good for my sanity. Everyone thought I had a screw or two lose anyway. Who knows what they would think if I had full on breakdown over a man I've only known for a month. Because I knew that would happen. I knew my heart would break when he left, and right now I was only making it worse. Making the fall hit me that much harder when it came time.

I pressed my lips against his, praying I would remember the taste of him mixed with whatever whiskey he must have drank before he came up here. His hands moved me, faster and faster until all we were was heavy breaths and loud moans. The closer I got; the more emotions welled inside of me. I wanted to prolong it, make it last forever. If it never ends, it can't be the last time. *Right?* With my hands placed firmly around his neck, and his on my hips, I rode until I had nothing left. Nothing but an agonizing moan that left me when we both tumbled over together. It was bliss. Beauty. *Perfection.*

Then it was over.

The next morning, I didn't just wake up to an empty bed. I woke up to an empty guest room. All of his things were gone. Not a trace left. At least he didn't make me empty promises. The one he did make, he kept. He never misguided me. He was upfront. Honest.

But my heart cracked anyway. Not because he left, but because he didn't even have the decency to tell me.

CHAPTER 37

Jace

I stared at the ceiling. Dodge had sent me a text last night that the house was ready, so I pulled a typical Jace Foster move and came back here in the middle of the night. After the tub, we laid in bed going over everything Laramie had told us before Camille fell asleep on my chest. I watched her sleep peacefully as I pressed my lips to her forehead. I should have known better than to break my one-night rule. It's always worked with any other woman. But I knew she wasn't just *any other* woman. I knew because I'd slept with Natalie a hundred times and it never felt anything close to this.

But my papers were right at my fingertips, and a job that I loved was waiting for me. It had been waiting for me. With one more kiss to her forehead I shifted out from under her and went into my room to pack my bags. A couple more weeks and I'd be cleared, and with a little hope, Meredith would be found. Timber Creek would just be a faint memory. A memory I might share over some beers with the guys back home one day. I was leaving.

But the longer I looked at her......the longer I wanted stay.

I had just poured a cup of coffee when I felt then energy in the room change. With a furrowed brow I looked over my shoulder just as Camille came across the squad room.

"Hey Cam." Rex held his arms out to hug her, but she walked straight past him, heading to where I stood in the kitchen.

Fuck.

I had prepared for her to be pissed. What I didn't prepare for was how hot she looked this angry. I sipped my coffee, watching every step she took until she walked right past me and into the hallway. Rex shrugged his shoulders when I looked at him for advice on how to approach her. She looked feral and I wanted to be careful enough she wouldn't blow up in front of her father. That's the last thing we needed right now. With a deep breath I followed behind her and into the hallway.

"I believe you owe me." She turned her stern eyes to me as I leaned up against the wall.

"Owe you?"

"If you're going to treat my house like some brothel, then I expect to at least be compensated."

"A brothel?" I asked, stunned.

"You scratched an itch, twice," she pointed out. "Then bolted." She poked her finger into my shoulder. "Without a fucking word."

"Camille... I didn't.."

"No, you did, Jace. You got what you wanted, then you left. Which is fine. I would prefer you go as far away from Timber Creek as possible. But what I'm not fine with is the fact I shared my home with you. My meals, my body, and you don't have enough respect to say thank you and let me know you would be leaving."

"I do respect you." She went to storm off, but I caught her by the arm. "I had to leave. I couldn't....." I clenched my jaw. This is not the place I wanted to have this conversation. Honestly, I didn't want to have it at all. I didn't want to admit the real reasons why I needed away from her. The reasons I avoided relationships. I wasn't worth the risk, because chances are I would end up disappointing her in the long run and she's the last person I would ever want to let down.

"You used me." She tossed her hands up. "I don't even know why I'm surprised."

"Woah." I tugged her closer to me. "I never used you. We both wanted it."

Her shoulders sagged as she looked away from me. I knew her well enough by now to know she was trying not to cry.

"Camille, look at me."

She shook her head, keeping her face fixated on the dark corner of the hallway. I glanced around, then tugged her a few steps farther until we were cloaked in the darkened hall.

"Look at me," I said again.

She looked up with tears rolling down both cheeks.

Shit. "Baby, don't cry." I wiped away a tear with my thumb before dropping my hand down to rest on the crook of her neck.

"I'm sorry." She ducked her head, pressing it into my chest. "You're right. I wanted it too. I shouldn't have said that. I knew where we stood from the beginning."

I leaned my chin down on the top of her head.

"I'm just letting old insecurities get the best of me." She sniffed, then picked up her head. "Ignore me. I'm an emotional wreck right now. I pretty sure I just ran over a baby rabbit on the way here and they were out of my favorite flowers at the market this morning."

I chuckled, but I didn't like the comment she made referring to old insecurities. Insecurities someone else instilled in her. "I'm sorry. It was a dick move. I should have told you." I admitted. I kissed the top of her hair. "You good?" I asked.

She nodded and peered around my shoulder.

I gripped her chin with my fingers, turning her so she was looking into my eyes. "Are you good?"

She searched my face before she gave me a small smile. "I will be."

I wanted to kiss her so fucking bad, but we already drew that line. The one we couldn't cross again.

"If you two are done, IT has a report ready," Adam said from the end of the hall.

We stepped apart and she smoothed down her shirt. "Well, I guess from now on we just keep things professional." She wiped underneath her eyes one more time before she started down the hall.

I watched her go with a deep ache in my chest.

Yeah. Professional.

CHAPTER 38

Camille

I did what I always did when I was hurting. I packed a bag, jumped in my jeep, then sent a text to my girls.

Me: I need y'all tonight. I'm on the way to Tilly's.

Tilly: Door's unlocked, Bekka is here already here.

Elle: On my way.

Whitley: Facetime me as soon as you get there.

My thoughts were jumbled. Peter, our technical analyst was able to find all the victims' profiles. Now it was just a matter of breaking them down and finding a common denominator. Somewhere or someone to start with. My mind kept revisiting Jace, then I would circle back to Laramie. *My golden angel.* Those three words sent a shiver over my entire body. I've heard those words before. I just needed to be sure. I needed another piece of the puzzle before I made any moves.

It took me longer than usual to get to Tilly's. It was snowing and the roads were getting spotty. After I parked in her driveway, I yanked my bag from the back seat and stomped up to her stairs. The door swung open before I even knocked and Tilly hurried me inside.

Elle only lived a few streets over, so all three girls looked at me with anxious expressions.

"What's going on?" Tilly asked.

I fell back into the couch with my elbow slung over my face. Tilly sat next to me, while Elle and Bekka sat on the love seat.

"It's detective dick. That's what's going on," Elle pointed out.

My eyes immediately filled with tears I had just spent thirty minutes drying up. I cried again when I walked past Jace's empty room. *Stupid.*

"Oh Cam, I'm sorry." Elle sat down the glass of wine she had in her hand before she stood, then wormed her way in between me and the arm of the couch.

"Well now I feel left out." Bekka stood up next and piled on the other end of the sofa by Tilly.

"We slept together," I confessed.

"I knew this was gonna happen." Elle wraps an arm around my shoulder.

"Twice," I added.

"I called it." Elle held up her hand. "Did I not?"

Tilly scrunched her nose. "She did."

"Well how was it?" Bekka asks. "You're crying, so I'm a little concerned."

"It was great. More than great actually." I tugged my sleeves over my hands. "We've just...it's been so rocky since we met and one minute I think he hates me then the next he's on his knees in my kitchen taking off my jeans. Now he just moved out without even saying a freaking thing."

"Back up. Jace Foster was on his knees?" Tilly asks with wide eyes.

"Yes and I will say I had no idea he was a giver." Memories of our clashing bodies filled my mind. "He was completely different than I expected."

"What happened?" Bekka leans back, peering around Tilly.

"We agreed it was one night. I was fine with that," I said.

"But?"

"But.... Well, it kind of happened again last night."

"I'm confused.....you wanted that too right?" Elle asked.

"Yes, but he's leaving!" I screeched. "He's going back to Mississippi in like three weeks. I would have been fine with one time. Just pushed it aside and forgot all about him, but then he got in the tub with me, his hands started to wander and before I knew it I was in his lap, riding...." I trialed off as I realized all the eyes that were on me were the size of saucers.

"Riding what!? For the love of all things holy please finish that sentence," Elle shrieked.

"Use your imagination, Elle," I deadpanned.

"So why can't y'all just have some fun while he's here?" Bekka looked at me like I was certifiably insane.

"Crap." Tilly's phone buzzes and she snatches it from the table. "It's Whit."

"We agreed it was best to not cross the professional line anymore," I stated with as much confidence in my voice as I could muster.

"Great. She's in love with him," Elle declared.

"Who's in love with who?" Whitley's voice filled the room and all I could see was her left nostril on the screen.

"Cami is in love with Jace," Bekka answers.

"Did I not teach you anything?" Whitley scolds. "Love is dead."

"Geez, Whit. Can you show a little mercy. Not all of us are sworn to never love again," Tilly snaps.

Whitley rolls her eyes and pops a Cheeto into her mouth.

"I'm not in love with him," I defend.

I'm not. I just like him. He can make my eyes roll back in my head and he has the sexiest laugh I've ever heard. That's it. It's not that I feel like an elephant is crushing my rib cage at the thought of him leaving. It's not like I wanted to literally die at the thought of him being with anyone else.

I can't love him. *Because he doesn't love me.*

"I hate to break it you sis, but I agree with Elle," Tilly says.

"Whose side are you on??" I gasped.

"I saw what happened at the bar." Elle crosses her legs. "The whole truck debacle."

"What truck debacle?" Tilly eyes me.

"Oh, Jace was pissed she was trying to leave with Dustin, so he ripped her out of the front seat and put her in his truck." Elle smiled. "He was livid."

"Damn...." Bekka mutters.

"Yeah....and I saw the kiss," Elle admits.

My cheeks blush, but then I stop, turning my head to face Elle. "Wait, how do you know? I thought you were in the bar?"

She nibbled on her lip. "Well...I guess I had one too many tequila shots. I threw up on Easton's boots, so he took the liberty of taking me home and putting me to bed. I was in his truck when your episode went down."

"Put you to bed?" I lifted a brow.

"Not like that." She narrows her eyes. "He's a freaking dad. Believe me, I felt like I was an eight-year-old in time out."

"Ohhh did he spank you?" Whitley waggled her brows.

Elle flipped her off. "Eat your weight in Cheetos, Whitley Harper."

Whitley barks out a laugh. "See girls, this is why I stay single."

"I am single," Elle hisses.

"I hate to jump on the band wagon, but I saw the hand thing at Thanksgiving." Whitley sighs.

"What hand thing?" I bit down on my lip after the question, trying not to give myself away.

I knew exactly what she meant. I thought my heart would beat straight out of my chest when he intertwined our fingers during the prayer.

"The point is I saw this shit coming." Whitley moved, laying back on her couch. "I saw how y'all watched each other all day. It was fucking creepy."

I moved my eyes down, pinning them on Tilly's fur rug. "None of that matters. He's leaving. He has a whole life in Mississippi. A career. We got it out of our systems and now we are...just..." I wanted to say friends but.... "Coworkers?"

"Are you asking?" Whitley laughed.

"So, what do you need?" Elle intervened.

"I just need y'all to tell me I'm fine, he's too old for me anyway and he's a world class asshole. Just give me wine, and let's watch a true crime documentary," I demanded.

"We can handle that." Tilly reached over and hugged me.

"Well, that's my cue. Good night girls. Cam, I love you. And even though I don't believe in the whole "love thing," I think you might be on to something."

I nodded as she blew me a kiss before hanging up.

"Alright. Let's see what we got. Bekka, get the wine." Tilly grabbed the remote, flipping on the TV.

It was paused on a football game.

"Is that Greyson's game from last week?" I peeked at Tilly from the corner of my eye.

She fumbled with the remote, changing the channel. "Yeah...I worked late that day, so I just recorded it." She cleared her throat.

"Yeah. I know you're such a big football fan," I joked.

She glared at me and I chuckled. Sounds like we all have issues. Except for Bekka. Her and Adam are golden.

"There's something else isn't there?" Tilly reaches out and grabs my hand.

"Yeah.... but I'm not sure yet. I need to be sure before I can tell you. I just need you to trust me." I squeezed her hand.

Her eyes searched my face. "Of course, I trust you."

I gave a half smile, then reached for the glass of wine Bekka handed me.

I was ready to forget about my problems.

Just for one night.

CHAPTER 39

Jace

I lifted my hand, knocking my knuckles against Easton's front door. It was late, and I felt like an asshole for doing this, but going to Adam was off the table. I highly doubt he would want to know exactly why I left his sister's house and the reasons leading up to it.

Easton opened the door with a surprised look on his face. "Jace, everything alright?"

"Not really. I just.... I would go to Adam, but..." I trailed off.

He waved a hand and opened the door. "No problem, man. Come in."

I stepped inside, just as little feet came bounding down the staircase. "Daddy, who's here?"

June stopped at the bottom, propping a hand on her hip. "Mr. Bossy."

I smiled. "Hi June."

Easton scooped her up. "It's past your bedtime bug." He kissed her check. "Her grandma filled her up on brownies this evening so she's a little wired."

"Frozen. I want Frozen daddy." June wiggled her way out of his arms and crawled onto the couch.

"Come watch it boss." She patted the couch cushion next to her.

"If that's ok with your dad."

Easton laughed. "Ok, we'll watch it in here, but you have to lay down with your blanket."

She smiled with a nod as she drug a raggedy blanket up from the floor. I plopped down on the cushion and without hesitation, she snuggled right up next to me. I placed my arm on the back of the couch, letting her get comfortable. I wasn't around kids much at all. I had no nieces or nephews and none of my friends had kids except Waylon and Hailey. Their son was only six months old when the shooting happened.

Easton turned on the movie, which zapped June's attention and he settled in the recliner next to the couch.

"You want to talk about it?" He asked.

I kept my eyes on the screen. "I'm not sure I know where to start."

He chuckled. "I guess we can start with the hard part first. Might as well rip off the band aid."

"I'm pretty sure I'm in love with her." I blinked, almost shocked at my own confession. I knew I was developing feelings, but I didn't know just how deep they had grown until tonight.

"Okay." He nodded.

"I'm going home in a few weeks." I glanced down at June, who's eyes were growing heavy. "I was trying to put some distance between us and I guess I went about it the wrong way." I let out a puff of air. "I know I went about it the wrong way," I corrected.

"You know she hasn't had the best experience with relationships." He met my eyes. "Stuart."

"Yeah," I scoffed. "We didn't officially meet, but I've had the pleasure."

"He's put her through some shit." He peers over to make sure June didn't hear. Which she didn't. She's now fast asleep, her head resting on my side. "You know he's like forty-two right?"

"Really?" I frowned.

"Yeah well...let's just say he's been playing games with her since we were sixteen."

My hackles rose. *Six fucking teen.*

"They didn't get together publicly until she turned eighteen. Richard was pissed, but what could he do? She was an adult. She had been struggling since her mom died, so he let her go. Kept his mouth shut as long as he could. We all did."

"And Adam?" I asked.

"It's came to blows between them more than once." He shook his head. "He manipulated her. Groomed her in my opinion. She was vulnerable and he used that to get into her head."

"I swear to God next time I see that piece of shit..." I growled.

"She finally cut the cord for good about a year ago. According to Elle. But he stills tries to play mind games. She's seeing through the bullshit now." He sat up, resting his elbows on his knees. "She's just scared, Jace."

My hands clenched. I wanted to strangle him for hurting her. "There's a lot more to it, Easton. Cap warned me."

"Richard is a good man. He's tough, but he loves his daughter and if he knows you're genuine he will understand."

I scrubbed a hand across my face. "He told me my release papers depended on it. That if I follow his rules, I'll get my career back."

"Which do you want more? The job? Or her?" He lifted a brow.

I knew the answer. I knew what I wanted more.

"This is the last thing I expected." I tilted my head back, looking up at the ceiling. "She was a fucking curve ball I didn't see coming.'"

"Sometimes the curve balls can be the best thing that ever happened to you." Easton's voice was quieter and I glanced over to see his eyes on his sleeping daughter. "We all have to make hard choices, Jace."

I watched his face, the way he scrunched his brow. It was obvious he had to make some hard choices in the past. Ones that changed his life. I don't know the story of June's mother, or why she wasn't in the picture, but I could tell he held a lot of that shit inside. I see it every time he looks at Elle.

"What did your choices cost you?" I asked.

His eyes meet mine again and he didn't have to answer, I knew. It cost him *her.*

And I wasn't sure if I was willing to do the same anymore.

Chapter 40

Camille

I heard my name being called. It whistled with the wind.

"Camille...he's coming."

I tried to move my arms, but I couldn't. They were weighted down. Heavy. It was dark, but I could feel him. I gasped for air just as his hand wrapped around my throat. His palm crushed against my windpipe, cutting off any air I had left in my lungs. Then it came. Just a small sliver of light, but it was enough to see the silver piece dangling above my face. The necklace. The coolness of the metal tipped my chin as he leaned in closer. His face was void. Black. I saw nothing but the outline of a cap. I strained to see his eyes. His lips. Anything. But all I could see was the cross pendent handing around his neck. My heart thudded wildly and my vision blurred.

"My golden angel," he whispered.

Then it all went black.

My eyes shot open, and I sucked in a ragged breath. My body darted up, unease slithering through every pore in my skin. My eyes bounced around, then I remembered I was in Tilly's guest room, which brought me a moment of relief. My hand swiped a piece of hair that was coated in sweat off of my forehead before I slung my feet to the carpet. It was different this time. The feeling. It wasn't Meredith he was taking this time.

It was me.

I needed to get back to the house. Check on my guests and let Achilles out. I had a lot on my mind. A lot of things to sort out in my head and I needed to play my cards right. A woman's life depended on it.

Dressed, I hustled downstairs to find Tilly making breakfast.

"Hey," I called out, but she didn't turn around.

She must not have her hearing aids in. I walked over to the bar and waited for her to face me. She smiled and pointed to her ears. I nodded and spoke slow so she could read my lips.

"I have to run home and take care of a few things. I need to go to the station later." I slid my purse and bag onto my shoulder. "Thanks for letting me stay."

She sat down her spatula, and walked around the bar. Her arms wrapped around my neck and I squeezed her tight. "Love you Cam," she whispered.

"Love you," I whispered back.

I couldn't place it, but the unwelcome feeling of fear spread across my chest. And judging by the way my sister hugged me, she felt it too.

Another week had almost gone by. There was something I needed to handle at the station and it wasn't the act itself that had me moving at a snail's pace. It was that I knew Jace would be there. Since he left, we've been distant. But that's the point. Neither of us wanted an attachment, for different reasons of course, but we had the same thing in mind. Keep things simple. We were putting up boundaries. Giving each other space. Keeping things work related. It was for the best.

My eyes closed as soon as I put my jeep in park in front of the station. I only took a moment before I pulled the lever, stepping out onto the snow-covered asphalt. When I entered the squad room it was busy as usual. Phones were ringing and uniforms were spread throughout the room. Jace was at his desk. A pen in hand, the cap resting between his lips. I realized I was jealous. Jealous his lips weren't on me but on crappy piece of plastic. *Well, that's a new low.* Being jealous of a writing utensil.

I blinked away the thought just as he lifted his gaze. His eyes caught mine and I could feel their intensity all the way across the room. I quickly looked away, striding past Myra and into the kitchen. I had brought a batch of banana nut muffins today. Or at least that's my excuse for being here.

I had just organized the counter when my dad stepped in. "Hey, sweetheart. I didn't know you were coming today."

His big arms lifted to hug me.

"Just dropping by. Made y'all some treats."

He sniffed the air. "You know I can't resist the banana nut."

I laughed. "Neither can Hollis. That's why I brought them."

"You better take him one. He's been buried in paperwork all day."
He squeezed my shoulder before he left.

I piled up two muffins on a napkin and headed to Hollis' office.

"I hate to interrupt," I said as I knocked on the frame of his open door.

He looked up from his papers and smiled. "Is that what I think it is?"

"Yes sir. Made fresh today." I stepped in, walking to the side of his desk.

"Thanks Cami." He picked one up, and took a large bite.

I crossed my arms and turned, admiring the pictures on his wall. His family. Him and my dad. The last department Christmas party. My eyes moved to one picture in particular. The air caught in my lungs. There it was. What I came here for.

"I'm gonna head out. Tell Trish I said hello," I said as I started out the door.

"Will do kiddo," he called out.

I was only a few steps out of his office when Easton came out of an interview room. "Cam, can you do me a favor? I'm out of my blank report sheets. Could you grab me a stack out of the supply closet? I got a guy waiting in here." He motioned with his head to the room behind him.

"Sure."

Crossing the room, I made a left down the hallway to the last door. I flipped on the light as I stepped in and went to the far shelf where all the documents were kept. I bent down to grab a stack when the door opened. My head whipped up and my stomach flipped inside out.

There he stood. Washed out jeans and a white button up.

Jace.

Chapter 41

Jace

I watched Camille's eyes flare. "Easton needed me to grab something," she said before she reached for a pile of papers.

"No, he doesn't. He asked you in here for me," I admitted.

She paused and turned her eyes one me. "Why?"

I started towards her. "I wanted to speak with you alone."

She tucked her hair behind her ears and crossed her arms. Like the motion was preparing her. Placing up her armor, guarding her heart from me. I could tell by the look on her face she was terrified. Not of me, but the way she felt about me. I took a few more steps until I was close enough to smell the citrus shampoo in her hair. There was no way I could be this close and not touch her.

My hand slid past her cheek and into her blonde strands. I tugged her forward until my forehead met hers. "Fuck, I missed you, Sunshine," I murmured.

I did. I had seen her in passing only a couple of times this week and to say I've been an irritable pain in the ass is an understatement. Even Rex told me I needed to get my shit together. Told me to quit being a pansy and admit to myself that I wanted her. Not just for a night or for two, but for as long as she would have me. Even if that meant I gave up my job in Mississippi.

"Jace." She looked up me with a helpless expression. "We agreed to be professional."

I shook my head. "I'm done being fucking professional. I'm done pretending this is just a job. That I'm only concerned about your well-being because I'm paid to." I slipped my hands farther into her hair, angling her face up to mine. "I'm done pretending I haven't wanted you since the first time I saw you in Adam's kitchen."

She gulped, tears forming around the blue of her eyes.

"I know you're scared." I leaned my forehead down again, resting it on hers. "I don't know what tomorrow holds. I don't know what's going to happen with my job, or if your father is gonna want to kill me when I tell him all of this, but I do know one thing." I paused, taking in a deep breath.

"And what's that, detective?" She whispered.

"You are where I want to be," I confessed.

A tear slid down her cheek. "You...you're serious?"

"I'd lay down my badge right fucking now if it meant I could kiss you."

She let out a sound that was a laugh mixed with a cry. "You better not." She closed her eyes and I wiped away a lone tear with my thumb.

"You mean it?" She whispered.

"Mean what, baby?" I asked.

"You want to be here? In Timber Creek?" Her hands lifted, curling around my biceps.

"Yeah. I mean it." I leaned in, hovering my lips over hers.

"That scares me to hear you say that out loud," she whispered.

Our noses danced; the closeness sent sensations straight to my groin. My fingers that were still buried in her hair flexed as she pushed up onto her toes, sealing her lips to mine. A groan left my throat as I opened my mouth, coaxing her with my tongue. My chest rumbled as she deepened the kiss and trailed her sharp nails up my arms, then around the back of my neck. One of her legs lifted and I caught it beneath her thigh, holding it to my hip. She grinded herself against me and my knees nearly buckled.

"Camille......" I groaned against her lips.

She moaned and it shot straight to my cock. It must have, because my brain was telling me it was a horrible idea to fuck her in this supply closet with her father and the rest of the PD just outside the door, but I wasn't thinking with my brain. My hands went to her leggings, ripping them down to her ankles in one tug.

"Turn around." My voice was hoarse. Strained. If I wasn't inside her in the next three seconds, I was going to lose my shit.

She obeyed, twisting around to place her palms flat against the small filing cabinets. I unbuckled my belt and released the button on my jeans, before tugging down my zipper. My jeans hung down on my thighs and I flipped up her shirt, gliding my hand up the length of her spine. Her back arched when my cock teased her entrance. Moving my shirt out of the way, I gripped myself, lining up before I plunged inside, burying myself as far as I could go.

She cried out as my head tilted back. I had never felt anything like the feeling I felt when I was inside of her. My hips surged forward, shoving her against the cabinets. Anyone one could walk in here at any moment. Catch me with the captain's daughter bent over the office equipment. But I didn't care.

I leaned forward, so my chest was flush against her back.

"Can you be quiet, Sunshine?" I asked, flicking my tongue against her ear lobe.

She moaned again as I kept a steady rhythm. I trailed my lips down the back of her neck, as my palms squeezed her hips, guiding her along my shaft. With one more thrust, I pulled myself out, and she whimpered in protest. I spun her around, hoisting her up onto the cabinets. I didn't enter her again immediately. I let my tip circle against her and I smirked, watching her pupils dilate.

"Jace, please..." Her teeth pressed into her bottom lip and it was hands down the sexiest thing I'd ever seen.

I reached down, pulling off her boot so I could slide her leggings off one leg.

"Wrap your legs around me, baby." I told her.

She quickly obliged and without wasting another second I was driving back into her. My thighs burned, but I never let up. I made a promise to her and I expected to watch every single expression on her pretty face when I made her fall apart. *Again.*

"Jace...right.. the..." the words died on her tongue when I felt her clamp down around me. Her lips parted and I silenced her scream with my mouth as she shook beneath me.

"Open your eyes," I breathed out.

Her eyes blinked open, and I jolted. One more deep thrust and tingles erupted from the base of my spine. Jumbled curses left me as I nuzzled my face in the crook of her neck, pouring out the last of my release.

When my muscles relaxed, I placed a kiss on her neck, then her shoulder before leaning up to meet her eyes.

"So." She swallowed through a shallow breath. "I guess this means we're friends?"

I slipped out of her, barking out a laugh as I did. "I think we both know we've never just been friends."

She smiled and jumped down off the cabinet. "I know what hooked you."

"And what's that?" I yanked up my jeans.

"My vocals," she mused.

"I would love nothing more than to wake up every morning to your vocals." I dropped a kiss on her temple as she adjusted her clothes.

She lifted a brow. "Expecting to move in already, detective?"

"I already told you. You're where I want to be." I reached out and snagged her by the waist. "If you'll have me."

"I guess you aren't so bad." She leaned up, placing a soft kiss on my lips. "You're grumpy.... but if you can do *that* to me every night." She wagged her eyebrows.

There was a quiet knock on the door, and she froze.

A throat cleared. "Just a public service announcement. You have about two minutes until Cap realizes you've been banging his daughter in the supply closet, Foster."

I chuckled and she giggled.

"We better get this over with." I moved a piece of hair from her face.

"Not yet. There's something I need to take care of first, ok?"

I frowned. "Everything ok?"

She smiled. "Everything is fine. I'll see you at home."

Home. It didn't matter if I was in Mississippi, or any other town across the United States. Home was wherever she was.

CHAPTER 42

Jace

I stepped out behind Easton, tucking my shirt into my jeans. "Thanks."

"You're welcome. I had to create a diversion," he said over his shoulder.

"Diversion?" We walked into the squad room and the first thing I saw was West with a bloody towel placed over his nose. "Damn, you punched him in the face?"

"Fucker had it coming."

"Jace, I got those documents you asked for." Myra slid up next to me, brushing her breast against my arm. She handed me the papers, fluttering her lashes as she did.

"Thanks Myra," I said without giving her a second glance.

She stood next to me for a moment, before she cleared her throat and stepped away. Camille came breezing by, narrowing her eyes at me as she hit the main door. I winked and she let a ghost of a smile hit her mouth.

"Where's Adam? I gotta check these over with him," I asked.

Easton tilts his chin towards the other side of the room. "He's in there with Cap, covering my ass for popping West."

"Thanks again," I said before I headed to my desk. I had almost reached my chair when my phone rang. *Hailey.* I held it in my hand, staring at her name as I continued to let it ring. This is the second time this week she's called and I'm still to chicken shit to answer. I shoved it back in my pocket and sat down.

I had Myra pull the forms to show who was in charge of the cases Camille had been digging into, and who was the one to sign off on them. If they were either closed completely, or marked cold. If I could talk to those officers it might give us better idea on where to start.

Adam came out of the office, with a pointed look aimed at Easton. "You need to let that shit go, East. You know he only talks about her to piss you off."

"I think he got the message. Her name comes out of his mouth again it won't just be his nose that's bleeding," Easton seethed from behind me.

I had a hunch who he was referring to, but I kept my mouth shut. "You got time to look these over?"

"Sure." Adam closed Cap's door and I followed him into the conference room.

I laid the folder down and settled in one of the black chairs. There were three in particular I wanted to check on, but there seemed to be others that could be beneficial to this case.

"Alright, victim one." I flipped open the folder and lifted the sheet of paper. "Officer who took the report was Hank Phelps. June of 2014." I scanned down the page. "Hollis is who signed it off as a cold case in June of 2015." My brow creased. Typically, the case is left open for three years before they were considered cold.

I handed the paper to Adam and went to the next. "Next one was reported in November of 2016. Officer Dallin took the report."

"He retired." Adam sat down the paper and clasped his hands in front of him on the table.

"Looks likes she was considered a run away. Case closed by Hollis." I glanced over at Adam.

I pulled the next. "March 2018. You took the report." I moved to the bottom of the page. "Hollis signed off."

"Let me see that." Adam took the paper from my hand. "I remember her. Chrissy Kirk. She left one morning to hike Piney Mountain but never came home."

"So, she was considered deceased?" I lifted a brow.

He stared at the paper for a moment. "Every one of these girls has the APP."

"We have three unsolved cases of missing women and one active case, all women who used this app." I tossed down the folder. "We have a serious problem here, Adam."

"Fuck." He pinched the bridge of his nose. "Camille was right." He dropped his hand. "We might have a serial on our hands."

"She thinks he's in law enforcement."

Adam froze. "It's not possible. We don't have dirty cops, Jace."

"Look I mean no disrespect, but you're really close to everyone in this town. It can alter your perception."

He stood, pacing back and forth on the thin carpet.

"We need to sit down with Hollis."

"It's not him," he barked.

"I didn't say it was." I pushed to my feet. "But it can't be a coincidence he's the one who closed all of these cases when another detective was overseeing."

"He's a lieutenant. He has that authority." Adam ran a hand through his hair. "I've known him since I was kid. It's not him."

I nodded. "Ok. Then let's get his input on these. See what he remembers."

We stepped out into the squad room and went straight to Hollis' office. I pushed through the door, but his chair was empty.

"Where's Hollis?" Adam called out.

"He left about twenty minutes ago. Said he had a family emergency," Rex hollered out.

I spun around to leave his office, when I froze mid step. My eyes hung on a picture frame mounted to the wall. "What the fuck?" I muttered.

"What's wrong?" Adam asked.

I pointed to the frame, anger coursing through every inch of my body. "Why the fuck is he in this picture?"

Adam looked confused. "That's his son."

Like a jigsaw puzzle, the pieces started to fall into place. I could see it on Adam's face.

"Adam!" Rex came jogging down the hall. "IT tracked the IP address. We got a name and location."

Adam looked at the black ink, before he cursed, raring his fist into the wall. "Motherfucker!"

I opened my mouth to speak when a head of blonde hair, matching Camille's stepped up behind Adam. Tilly tapped him on the shoulder then her hands were moving. She was frantic, her eyes welling with tears as she signed to us both.

"Tilly you're moving too fast, slow down." Adam grabbed her by the shoulders.

Her teeth clenched together and she shook her head. "It's Camille," she cried.

At her name I immediately stepped up to her. "What's wrong?"

"I don't know." Her hand went to her chest. "I can feel it. Something's not right." She lifted her phone from her coat pocket. "She sent me this text and I came straight here."

Cami: I'm going to Piny State Park. If you don't hear from me in one hour. Go to the station.

Adam and I met eyes.

She knows it's him.

CHAPTER 43

Camille

I stood at the far east end of the park entrance. I knew this spot well. Just like he did. Leaning up against my jeep, I watched as headlights flashed across the dark trees, then past me. He parked, then stepped out with that cunning smile he always had visible. With one long leg in front of the other he strode towards me.

"Miss me baby?" He husked.

I bit the inside of my cheek, giving him nothing but a blank stare. When his cologne hit me, I wanted to gag. I used to love it. Felt comforted by it, now, it just makes me sick.

His hands shot out, gripping my face in his palms. "You always come back to me." He leaned in and I turned my face, causing his lips to land against my cheek. "My golden angel," he whispered against me.

I cringed. Like I'm something special to him. I never was. The only reason I knew he would come here is because it "means something" to him. It's where he used to bring me. *Where he used me.*

"It's over Stuart," I hissed.

"We're never over," he whispered harshly.

I raised my palms, planting them against his chest before I shoved him away from me. "You." I gritted my teeth. "It's been you the whole time."

He had the nerve to look hurt by my accusation. The theatrics this man could perform still floors me.

"I told you about my dreams. You made me out to be crazy. Mentally unstable!" I shook my head. "You used me! Manipulated me to think something was wrong with me. That you were the only one who could..."

My throat was swelling with tears, but I refused to cry. I have cried enough over him through the years. I cried the first time he felt me up when I was sixteen. When he slid my panties down my legs and told me I was special. That *he* was the only one who ever saw me. I cried again when he told me he loved me. That there was nothing inappropriate with our relationship. *Even though he was my therapist.* He was supposed to be helping me learn to navigate through life with the death of a parent. I kept it a secret. Never told a soul until I graduated and acted like it had just happened. Like he wooed me over a family dinner at my parent's house one night. I know my father didn't approve, but Hollis was his best friend, and Stuart was good at making you do things you didn't want to. Giving you a false sense of security.

I cried when I walked in on him fucking a random girl in our bedroom after I moved in with him when I was nineteen. I cried when he told me that love required acceptance and I had to accept who he was. *Accept* when he didn't come home until two in the morning, smelling like another woman's perfume. I had to *accept* that even though he had sex with them, he never loved them like he loved me.

I was done crying. I was done a year and a half ago when I broke things off for good. Moved out to Piper Lake and was determined to heal from all the shit he had put in my head. He had me convinced no one would love me. Not with my "mental illness." I was dumb enough to believe it. *Vulnerable. Sad. Impressionable.* But I wasn't anymore. I was so much stronger than that scared girl searching for answers to things she didn't understand. Why her mother got cancer. Why she was born healthy and her sister wasn't. Why she had dreams that haunted her for years.

"You sound crazy, Camille," he scoffs.

I laughed. "I'm the crazy one? I'm not the one kidnapping women, Stuart!" I screamed. "What did you do to them? Where is Meredith!"

My hands were shaking. I was angry. So angry I didn't see it before. So angry he played me. *And I allowed it.*

"That's enough. What the hell has gotten into you?" He stormed towards me.

"Don't you touch me." I held up a hand. "You make me sick."

His tongue came out, swiping over his bottom lip. "I don't believe I made you sick when you would fuck me in the front seat of my car." He pointed. "Right under that tree over there."

It was twisted, but I thought that's what I had to do to deserve his love. Give him my body. All I ever got was an unfinished orgasm and even more emotional trauma.

"You're pathetic," I spat.

"Watch your mouth." He lunged forward, gripping my jaw so hard I knew it would bruise. "You think you can run that pretty little mouth just because you're whoring around with that new detective?"

His lip curled up, snarling at me as he put more pressure on my jaw, causing my teeth to scrape against my lip. I could taste the blood as it trickled into my mouth.

"I got news for you Angel." He leaned in, his tongue tracing the tear that ran down my cheek. "If I can't have you, no one can."

His other hand lifted in my peripheral, then it all when black.

My last though was, *where are they? They should have been here by now.*

It's too late.

CHAPTER 44

Jace

"What's going on out here!" Cap barks as he steps out of his office.

"It's Stuart, dad." Adam shoves the paper at his chest. "The IP address connected to all four women trace back to him."

Cap's shoulders stiffen as he reads it. He clenched the paper between his finger. "I should have handled him when I had the chance."

"Hollis knows," Adam croaks. "He's been covering up for him."

I can see the anguish written all over his face. This is his best friend. Someone he trusted.

"Find them both," he growls. "I want answers."

"We gotta get to Camille." I look over at Adam. "I think she knows it's him. We find him, we find her."

"Easton! Rex!" Captain Harper whistles, gaining their attention. He glances back at us. "You two go. I'm sending backup. Tilly you stay here."

Not five minutes later we're loaded in Adam's truck.

"Why the hell didn't I know Stuart was Hollis' son?" I roared as Adam damn near rolled us turning onto the main road.

"I didn't even think to mention it. He and Camille have been estranged for a while. Hollis stays out of it, so does dad. They are both adults." Adam's hands gripped the steering wheel. "I always thought something was off with him." He shook his head. "I mean, what kind of therapist ends up dating their fucking patient? Even if she is the daughter of your dad's best friend."

Hold up. "Her fucking therapist?" I shouted. I thought back to what Easton had said. "When did she start seeing him as her therapist?"

"After mom died. She was sixteen." Adam turns left, skidding across the slick asphalt.

My hand gripped the hand rest so hard I thought I'd break it off. "I'm gonna fucking kill him."

"Jace, I don't know what's going on with you and Cami..."

"I love her," I interrupted.

It came out smoothly. Like a known fact. There was no question about it. Not anymore.

He was quiet for a brief second before he nodded. "I figured."

I let my head fall back and I closed my eyes.

"My gut told me it was him that night. I should have listened," Adam muttered.

"What night?" I asked rolling my head to the side.

"When the last woman went missing, Camille had one of her dreams. She tried to talk to dad, but he wasn't buying it." He pressed harder on the gas. "She decided to go off on her own. She thought she knew where the girl was. My father warned her to stay put. The roads were icy and he didn't think it was safe for her to be out." I leaned up as soon as I saw the Piney State Park sign. "I guess she was getting too close because when she was almost to the location someone ran her off of the road. Her car was caught down in a ravine. We didn't know anything had happened until the next day when Stuart just *happened* to find her."

"Convenient."

"Yeah. Her car wasn't visible from the road, so it made me wonder how he knew where to find her. They weren't even together anymore." We pulled into the parking area just to the left of the entrance. "She was in the hospital for three days until she finally woke up."

"Yeah. I'm gonna fucking kill him," I reiterated.

There were no other cars in sight. She could be anywhere. I jumped out, my boots crunching against the snow as we scanned the area.

"Shit, there!" Adam yelled. "I can see the hood of her jeep!"

I jogged behind him as we moved through the trees until we reached the side parking area of the park. Her jeep was the only vehicle there. I took off in a sprint, reaching the driver side door before Adam. It was empty. Dread coursed through my limbs as I peered inside to see her purse and phone in the seat.

"Fuck!" I slammed the door. "He's got her." My hands lifted, bracing on the top of my head as I inhaled.

Adam's phone rang, startling the silence of the mountains. "East?" He answered.

He listened intently, before nodding his head towards the truck. "We're on the way."

He hung up, sliding his phone back into his coat pocket. "Stuart's neighbor just called in and reported a disturbance."

Sweat was forming on my brow as we jumped back into the truck. I could barely breath. Barely fucking think. All I knew was we had to get there. Fast.

He's taken enough from her.

CHAPTER 45

Camille

My eyelids were heavy, but I peeled them open. I could see her. She was huddled in the corner. A gag in her mouth. It was dark. Musty. The smell of mold hit my nostrils as I inhaled. Her eyes widened as she looked at me, tears forming as she tried to scream through the cloth lodged in her mouth. I took a step, but I couldn't move. Why can't I move? Something heavy was weighing me down.

"I'm here." The whisper was shaky. Scared. "I'm right here, Camille."

"Wake up, Angel."

Bile rose in my throat at the voice. My eyes cracked open, and I saw a familiar painting on the wall. I knew where I was. I was in his house.

His hand ran through my hair. "There you are." He grinned.

I jerked my head away from his touch, which caused a throbbing sensation at the back of my skull.

"Careful. You may have a concussion." He reached across a coffee table. That's when I realized I was on his couch. "Take these."

He opened his hand revealing two blue pills.

"No," I croaked. "I'm not taking anything."

His eyes flared. "Camille, you're taking the pills. I didn't mean to hurt you. But you were talking crazy."

My hand flattened against the couch cushion and I pushed myself to a sitting position. "I said no."

He calmly set the pills on the table, then turned to face me with a demeanor I'd seen a hundred times. That glazed look that would pass his eyes when he couldn't control me. He was up for a hell of a fight. I wouldn't back down anymore. I refused to cower to his abuse.

"After all I've done for you." His tone was laced with distain. "You selfish little bitch."

My head felt hazy, but I tried to push through it. I tried to find a way to beat him at his own game. My eyes lowered, catching on a shiny object on the table. *It was a needle.* A syringe. He followed my panicked gaze and smirked.

"I brought this as backup. In case you misbehaved." He raised a hand and tucked a piece of hair behind by ear. "Are you going to behave, Angel?"

Four seconds ago, I was a bitch? He's deranged.

This was it. I should have learned a thing or two from him by now. How to play the part to get what I wanted. I let my shoulders relax, and mustered up all the strength I had remaining.

"Yes. I'll behave."

His smile was eerily slow spreading. "You better thank me properly for allowing you back into my home."

I had to ignore the nausea thrashing inside of me. But I knew one thing about Stuart, he was easily distracted. I raised up, planting my knees onto the leather sofa so I could be eye level with him as he sat on the coffee table across from me. "What would you like for me to do?" I tilted my head, a coy and misleading smile pulling at my lips.

"You know exactly what I like."

His hands grabbed at my breasts and I bit down on my lip to keep the sob from escaping my throat.

"I missed you.... those other women.....they're not like you." His hands moved under my shirt, lifting it up to expose my bra.

"Did you love those other women? The women you took?" I asked as I ran my hand through his hair.

"No." His mouth went to my skin. "I only loved you. Those girls never meant anything to me."

Tears slid down my cheeks as I swallowed and prepared for my next words. "I want you."

He pulled back and smiled, moving me aside so he could sit on the couch. He tugged me onto his lap and I straddled his legs. Memories of this exact position flooded me and I wanted to scream. I hated myself for what I had done. More tears came as I arched my back to let him nuzzle his face between my breasts.

"You fucked that detective," he said against me.

It wasn't a question. It was a statement.

"I did," I admitted.

I leaned farther back. Letting him drag his mouth down my upper abdomen.

"He will never love you like me," he said. "Not when he knows what you are, Camille."

I let my head fall back, just enough that I could see to my left. I stretched out my arm quickly, before grasping the syringe in my palm. His mouth was still on me. Running his disgusting tongue along my bellybutton.

"I have a confession," I whispered. I lifted his head with my free hand to look into his eyes. "You're right. His love is nothing like yours."

Before he could reply, I raised my left hand, jamming the needle into the side of his neck.

"And I've never loved you like I love him," I gritted out.

His reaction was slow, but once he realized what I had done, he lunged forward, tackling me against the coffee table that buckled beneath our weight. He jerked the need needle out of his neck before his hands went to wrap around my throat. I screamed as loud as I could, kicking at any part of him that I could reach.

His eyes were pure evil as he squeezed harder and harder, cutting off my air supply. I yanked at his wrist, gasping for any amount of air possible. Frantically, my hands clawed at the buttons on his shirt. When my fingers caught below his collar, I yanked, and a sliver chain tumbled out, revealing a cross dangling in front of my blurring vision.

My dream.

"I already told you. If I can't have you, no one can," he hissed with another round of increased pressure to my throat.

I was fading. Weakening by the second, praying whatever liquid that was in that syringe would be taking affect sooner rather than later.

Then I heard a voice. A voice that pulled his attention and his grip loosened the tiniest of a fraction.

My heart lurched.

It was Hollis.

CHAPTER 46

Jace

When we slid into Stuart's driveway, Easton and Rex were just stepping out of the squad car along with Hollis who was halfway up the driveway.

"Hollis!" Adam bellowed.

I knew this wasn't going to be good. This was too personal for everyone. Too many emotions. *Too much anger.*

"You sorry motherfucker!" Adam had reached Hollis before any of us could stop him.

His fist flew into Hollis' jaw, splattering blood across the snow.

"Adam, please," Hollis groaned after he regained his footing.

"You knew! You knew he was doing it the whole time!" Adam yelled.

Hollis shook his head. "No. Not the whole time...." He wiped the blood from his mouth. "He's my son."

"I don't give a shit who he is." Adam winds back to hit him again, but Easton caught him around the shoulders.

They could beat the shit out of each other for all I care, I was here to get my girl. My wrath could be delivered later.

"Let me go in. Please Jace. He's a not well....he's not himself right now and he won't listen to anyone but me." Hollis turned; his breaths heavy as he adjusted his holster.

I watched his expressions. You could clearly see he was concerned. Not just for Camille, but for his son's state of mind.

"You've got two minutes tops." I pointed. "He lays a fucking hand on her I swear Hollis, I'll kill him."

"He was never supposed to hurt her. He promised." He gulped.

"When this is all done, you and I are going to have a talk, too."

He nodded as Adam continued to rant from behind me. My attention flew to the end of the drive when Cap came charging out of his truck.

"Where is she!!" He barked.

"Rex!" I called out. "Handle him."

I pointed at our severely irate captain before I turned to head for the house. Hollis had already gone inside and I heard a strangled scream. It was her. The pain and fear in her voice sent a jolt straight to my chest. I could hear Hollis talking in a raised voice, but the words were muffled by the anger boiling inside of me. I pushed through the front door, following the voices to the back of the house.

"Son, you don't want to do this. You swore you would never hurt her," Hollis pleaded.

I could hear, but I couldn't see yet. My hands shook with every second that passed that I didn't have eyes on her. I finally reached Hollis' back.

"Let her go. You don't want to hurt her," he said again.

My eyes landed on Stuart who was straddling Camille on the floor in a pile of broken wood with his hands around her throat.

Stuart glanced up. "I would never...." His face was red. Angry and rigid. "She belongs to me," he gritted out.

Like hell she does.

Camille was gasping, yanking at his wrists, but her movements began to slow, turning sluggish.

"We just want to be sure she's ok. If she's ok you can stay with her." Hollis took a step forward. His eyes quickly darted to me as he did.

Stuart looked down at Camille, and loosened his hold. When his hands fell from her throat she sucked in a ragged breath, coughing as she gulped the oxygen her body needed.

"We need to check her out. You need to let her up," Hollis said calmly.

My hand was positioned on my weapon that was strapped to my hip. I was ready. One wrong move and I would send this piece of shit straight to hell.

He slowly leaned back on his heels, allowing Camille to roll over. Her eyes met mine and a sob poured out.

"Just stay there, Stuart." Hollis held up his hand.

Camille scrambled to her knees, still breathing deep as she did.

"Come to me, Sunshine," I said as she raised to her feet.

Stuart's crazed eyes moved over to me, then back to her as she stood. Something in his expressions was off. Hollis must have sensed it too because his hand traveled to his weapon. I reached out my hand just as my eyes caught on the small movement. It was subtle, but I saw the glint of the barrel before I saw Stuart lift his hand, pointing a gun he pulled from the back of his jeans straight at Camille's back.

"She's mine," he seethed.

Like a strike of lightening, it was quick, but it felt like I watched in slow motion. Stuart's gun raised, Hollis pulled his weapon free, and I pulled mine just as I rushed forward to cover Camille.

Flashes of Waylon hit me as I stepped forward, remembering the night I could have saved him. My finger pressed the trigger, but two shots rang out. Stuart's limp hand dropped the gun, and he fell back onto the couch with a bullet wound in the front of his forehead. I felt relief, then immediate fear when Camille cried out from where she had fallen on the ground in a puddle of blood.

Not again. This can't be happening again.

CHAPTER 47

Jace

There could have been a million people in the room, but it was silent. I fell to my knees, my hands reaching for Camille's crumpled body on the floor. Blood pooled beneath her and a gurgled sound I never knew I could even make broke as I turned her to me so I could inspect her wound. The blood was coming from her lower back and I pressed my palm against it to try to stop the bleeding.

"I need a medic now!!!!" I shouted at Adam who was placing a set of cuffs on Hollis.

"She's..." Camille's voice was almost nonexistent, but she was trying to talk. "Here."

"What?" I lifted her head with my other hand so I could get closer.

"Mered...th." She gasped and her eyes fell closed.

"Keep your eyes open. I need you to keep looking at me."

I felt a presence. Easton appeared next to me with a hand on my shoulder. "They're coming. Medics are on the way."

Camille cracked her eyes open, but she was struggling. She was losing a lot of blood and the pressure I was applying wasn't going to work much longer.

"She's saying Meredith is here. We need to search the house." He immediately called to Rex and they alerted the other officers.

Chaos continued to erupt around us, but I stayed in place, holding her limp body in my arms. Her eyes went to fall closed again.

"Come on, baby. Please you have to fight it. Keep them open. Hang on to my voice," I pleaded.

I was watching the life dissolve straight from her eyes. I held on tighter. Applied more pressure.

"Where the fuck are they!" I roared.

"Jace. Where's she hit?" Cap kneeled down next to me, placing his hand on her forehead to push her hair back. "Camille, hang on sweetheart." His voice cracked.

It seemed like hours before the paramedics arrived.

I leaned down, landing a kiss at the corner of her mouth. "Don't give up on me, baby."

"Jace, they're here," Cap said.

I closed my eyes. I didn't want to let her go. What if this is the last time I ever got to hold her?

"Jace." I felt his hand on my shoulder. "You have to let her go so they can get to her."

I gave her one last kiss before I let the paramedics take her from my arms.

"I'll take him to hospital; you ride with her." Adam said to his dad as they extended the stretcher and started to wheel her out of the house.

Cap nodded and I noted the panic in his eyes. He was our leader. Always in control and had his emotions in check. But this was his daughter and his mask was slipping.

"Easton is handling Hollis," Adam added.

"All I'm worried about is her," Cap said as he climbed into the back of the ambulance.

The doors shut and with flashing red lights they tore out of the driveway. Adam and I jumped into his truck and followed the sirens all the way up to the emergency room doors in complete silence.

Three hours. That's how long I had been pacing the empty halls of the hospital. They took her straight back to surgery when we got here and we haven't received any updates. Tilly has been a complete wreck. Elle has zoned out like a zombie, and Adam and Richard are in no better shape than me.

"Whitley is about to board the plane," Bekka informed us.

She was the only one here who was holding it together. "I'll go grab us some coffees."

"I'll go with you." Adam hauled to his feet. "Til, come on."

She stood, wiping away a tear as she did. When they started down the hall Easton appeared. He looked exhausted, which I'm sure he was. He was dealing with all of the other bullshit while we were here. Elle let out a light sob and turned her face away from him when he made it to us.

"How is she?" He asked.

"No news yet. She's in surgery." Cap removed his hat and sat it in the chair next to him.

Easton glanced over at Elle who was still trying to hide her emotion. When he looked back at me I could see in his eyes he was asking me if she was ok.

I shook my head no. None of us were ok.

"Ellie, come on." He walked over and offered his hand to her.

"I'm fine," she croaked.

He lowered down in front of her and spoke in a low voice. She finally agreed and they left me and Cap alone in the waiting area.

I leaned over in my chair, dropping my forearms on my knees. I knew this conversation needed to happen. I wasn't sure if this was the time or place, but I needed something to fill the silence.

"I disobeyed your orders," I admitted. "You gave me one rule, and I broke it."

He kept silent as I continued.

"If you want to hold my release papers, or tell Chief Ward I'm a shit detective who can't stay in line and be trusted that's fine. I'll take the hit. I would give up my job. My career that has consumed me for the last ten years if she asked me to. I know my actions were disrespectful to you, but I never disrespected her. I would never do anything to hurt her." I leaned up, turning so I was looking directly in his eyes. "I love your daughter."

His expression wasn't of surprise or even anger. It was almost as if he was saying, *I've been waiting for you to tell me.* He lifted his leg, placing his ankle over his knee.

"I kind of caught on to that." He lifted a brow. "I was just waiting to see if you were man enough to tell me."

I blew out a breath. "I can tell you it was definitely something I didn't plan and I fought like hell against it at first, but she's..."

"She's a lot like her mother." He smiled, but his eyes grew glassy. "It nearly killed me losing, Dana. Camille reminds me so much of her. Strong willed. She's different than my other children. Not that I love her any more or less. She just had a different spirit. It scared me because I didn't know how to understand it. We were all grieving...." He let out a deep breath. "I blame myself for Stuart. I should have paid more attention. I should have known she just needed someone to believe her. I basically pushed her right to him."

"It isn't your fault."

"She was always the one to lift us up though. Even when she was going through hell.....she was always calming."

"I know what you mean."

And I did. She calmed whatever storm I had inside of me since the day my dad died. I wanted to make him proud. Be the kind of man and officer he was, but I only seemed to let down the people I cared about. I was angry at myself for disappointing Natalie, but I was even more angry at myself for not realizing sooner the truth about our relationship. *She just wasn't the one.* I was angry at myself when my actions cost my best friend his life. I've been so fucking angry. *Carried so much guilt.* Until she came marching through my life with a light I desperately needed.

"She's gonna make it," he declared. "She's too strong not to."

I prayed she did. Because if she didn't, I'd die right along with her.

CHAPTER 48

Camille

My back was killing me and I really needed to pee. My eyes peeled open, shutting abruptly when a bright light through a window almost blinded me. Achilles probably needed go outside, so I reached for the covers. I went to lean up when a sharp pain shot across my left side.

"Easy, Cam." I heard Tilly's voice and I was confused on why she would be at my house this early in the morning. "You have to stay in bed."

"I need to pee," I groaned.

I opened my eyes again and the first thing I saw was a small tv mounted on the wall that was definitely not mine. I frowned, then looked around the room. I was not at home. I was in the hospital. *What the hell?*

"Why am I....?" I began, but my words fell short.

Stuart. The park. The house. The gun. "What happened? Where is he?" I whispered.

She reached out to clasp my hand. "He's gone Cami. And you're safe."

"But Meredith!" I leaned up, wincing at the pain. "Is she alive? Did they find her?"

Tilly's eyes glistened with pride. "They found her. She's alive."

"Where?" I was able to reposition myself higher on the pillow.

"He had a room underground in his garage. She was bruised up a little bit, but she's ok." She smiled.

Voices grew louder as Whitley, Elle, and Bekka stopped in front of the open door to my room.

"I don't care how "heathy" they claim it is. This food is shit. I'm contacting hospital management." Whitley was in her natural state. *Boss babe.*

"I would kill for some jello right about now," I said.

All three jerked their heads in my direction. I smiled at the astonishment that painted their features.

"You're awake!" Elle darted towards me first, then Whitley and Bekka.

"It feels like every time I come home it's because you ended up in this place." Whitley motioned to the room. "Next time can we do like, I don't know, prison? You can at least get cigarettes."

I laughed. Whitley always used humor to hide her real feelings. I knew she was scared by the way her hand slightly shook when she tugged at her workout jacket.

"I'll see what I can do." I held up my arms, signaling I needed a hug.

She walked around the side of the bed just as Adam and my dad came in.

"She's decided to join us." My dad's smile was tight, but only because I knew he was holding back his tears. His eyes held so much sorrow. I knew he was sorry for not believing me. Sorry for so many things that he thought were his responsibility.

"Like I would miss Christmas. You know it's my favorite holiday. Plus, who's going to make sure the ornaments are appropriately distributed," I teased to lighten the mood.

"I forgot about Christmas. When is it? A week or so?" Whitley asked.

"Yeah, you might as well stay. You're just gonna have to fly right back," Adam said as he wrapped an arm around Bekka.

"Let's set aside Christmas for the moment. We need to focus on getting Camille healed and healthy." Dad used his "work voice" as I called it. All stern and orderly.

"Yes sir," I answered.

He shook his head as he shewed Tilly out of the way so he could kiss my forehead. "Love you."

"Love you too dad."

I didn't know the full extent to my injuries yet, but at the moment I was just happy to have everyone here. To have all of the people I loved in one place. But someone was missing. Actually, two someone's.

Where is he?

Tilly caught my eye. "He went to take care of Achilles. Nayna went with him."

I closed my eyes and tilted my head back. "Why on earth would you let Nayna in a confined space with him?"

Whitley laughed. "I can't wait to hear all about it when he gets back."

A figure stepped into the door frame. Just like always, my breathing altered. It always did when he entered a room. Jace stared at me. His eyes full of relief and his hand held a bouquet of tiny blue flowers.

The ones that match his eyes. My favorite.

CHAPTER 49

Jace

She was awake. *Alive.* A wave of emotion hit me and I had to choke back the urge to cry. I wasn't a crier. The last time I cried was at my dad's funeral. I was seven years old.

"Let's give them a minute." Cap gave his children a pointed look and they filed out of the room.

I made sure to stop and get her flowers. I wanted them to be by her bed when she woke up, but I think I like the idea of me giving them to her better now that she's looking at me the way she is.

"Hey." I cleared my throat as I stepped into the room and closed the door behind me.

"Hi," she said quietly.

I laid down the flowers and took a seat next to her on the edge of the bed.

"How was the car ride with Nayna?" She asked with a slightly terrified expression.

I pinched the bridge of my nose.

"That bad? I'm so sorry. She can be a little overwhelming," she apologized.

"Well, I'm now subscribed to monthly shipments of "life changing" lubricant. Those were her words," I pointed out.

"Monthly subscription?!" She shrilled.

"I didn't know what do to do. She kept explaining all the "benefits" so I just gave her my credit card before she started showing me YouTube videos."

She laughed out loud and covered her face when she snorted. I didn't even realize until this moment how much I missed her laugh. I never wanted to live without it.

"I love you," she said as her hands dropped and tears pooled in her eyes.

I intertwined my fingers with hers and brought her hand up to my lips, pressing a kiss to her knuckles. "I love you too, Sunshine. So fucking much."

I rose from the bed so I could kiss her. Her small hands framed my face and I could taste the tears that continued to fall. "No more tears," I whispered. "I'm not going anywhere."

She nodded then pulled away to look at me. "I'm sorry I went on my own. I just needed to be sure. I had to face him."

"And I'm so proud of you for that. For facing your demons." I gripped her chin lightly with my fingers. "But don't ever scare me like that again."

"I'm sorry," she whispered.

"As for Stuart. He's where he belongs. In the morgue." I kissed her again. "I promise I will spend the rest of my life making sure you know exactly what you mean to me. Exactly how much I love you. I plan to give back every single thing he took from you." I sat back down next to her. "This is exactly where I'm supposed to be."

"In Timber Creek?" She asked.

"With you."

Six weeks later

"So, she just didn't show up?" Camille asks from the passenger seat.

I had yet to tell her about Natalie. Not because I wanted to hide that I had been engaged, or hide my relationship with her. Truth be told I was embarrassed. It was a big hit to the ego, but after knowing all of her pain and the truth about her and Stuart, I felt it was time to share mine.

"Nope," I answered as I turned on my blinker.

Camille crossed her arms and shook her head. "Have you spoken to her?"

"Once. It was the day after. Haven't heard from her since." I shrugged.

"Where is she now?"

"Baby, I don't know. I just told you I haven't spoke to her in almost two years." I reached over to massage the back of her neck.

"I'm guessing you don't happen to have her license plate number?"

I laughed. "No, and you're not getting Adam to look her up either."

She rolled her eyes. "Sounds like she needs a swift kick in the ass. That, and I would like to thank her."

"Have I told you I love you today?" I asked as we pulled into the parking lot.

"You may have, but I could use a reminder." She grinned and leaned over the console of my truck when we parked.

I guided her to my mouth with the hand that was still on her neck. "I love you."

"I love you too, detective."

My chest grumbled at the phrase. She usually only called me that when we were naked and now was not the time for me to have a tent in my pants. I kissed her one more time before I pulled away and adjusted my myself.

"You ready?" She asked.

I blew out a breath as I looked at the building that was holding the Memorial to honor Waylon and three other officers, myself included, that were on the case together that day.

"Yeah. I'm ready."

CHAPTER 50

Camille

I watched with so much pride as Jace stood on stage. It took a lot of convincing on my part for him to be here, but he made the ultimate decision and I truly believe it's his first step to healing. Hailey had been calling him for weeks to try to talk him into attending. It was only when Chief Ward called that he finally agreed.

I had no idea what the case was. I just knew that the bust went wrong and two officers lost their lives while the others were injured. Regardless, they managed to save almost eighty-five children from human trafficking. It was huge for the state of Mississippi and many cases were brought full circle and parents were able to have some form of closure. Jace accepted his medal and the entire crowd paid their respects by a standing round of applause. A lovely sideshow and tribute were given to Waylon and the other officer who sacrificed their lives to save these beautiful children.

After the ceremony we were lingering in the parking lot when a woman with long black hair approached. She carried a smiling baby boy on her hip and I knew without even asking this was Hailey.

"Jace." She smiled and reached out her free arm to hug him. "How are you? It's good to see you."

"I'm good." After the embrace he wrapped an arm around my waist. "Hailey, this is Camille."

Her smile was warm as she held out her hand. "It's nice to meet you."

"Likewise." I returned the smile. "And who is this handsome fellow?"

"This is Jennings." She bounced him and he smiled a gummy smile.

My fingers lightly pinched at his chubby thighs. "Hi there, Jennings."

He laughed, cooing nonsense at my greeting.

"How long are y'all in town? I'd love to catch up," she asked.

"We have to head back this evening. We have a retirement party to attend tomorrow night. We have a long drive ahead of us," Jace said as his hand captured mine.

"Well, please don't be a stranger. We miss you and I would love to get to know the woman that is responsible for taming Jace Foster." She winked.

He laughed. "I promise, I'll keep in touch."

"Good." She hugged him again. "Waylon would be proud of you, Jace."

He nodded, before giving Jennings a tug on his curly hair. "Take care Hailey."

The entire ride home his demeanor was different. He seemed lighter. Like a heavy weight had lifted and he was able to breathe again. I felt the same. The day they put Stuart into the ground I could breathe for the first time. A good solid breath. Meredith was recovering and they were able to find the remains of the other three women. They were laid to rest with a proper funeral and their lives were celebrated. *Honored.* Hollis was charged with obstruction of justice and tampering with evidence. I know it hurt my father. Not just the betrayal he felt as a friend, but as a fellow officer. As a man of the law. Fortunately, with Hollis doing time, Adam was promoted to his position and Jace was able to be hired on as a full-time detective. We were both choosing to leave our pain in the past. Begin with a fresh start, and I have never been more excited for the future than I was right now. *With him.*

"How does it feel to be a retired old man?" Adam asked Hank.

"Who you calling old? I can still run circles around your ass," Hank grumbled before he lifted his beer mug to his burly mustache.

The second floor of The Peak was reserved for Hank's retirement party. We had cake, food, and of course, live music. Hank decided this last case with Meredith was the one to leave on. He wanted to go out on a good one. One where justice was served.

I carefully watched Jace from my spot at the table as he was in deep conversation with Rex. We had just occupied the third stall in the bathroom and even though he pulled through on his promise once again, I was still squirming in my seat at the possibility of another when we got home.

Tilly had just brought us a round of shots when my phone buzzed.

Elle: Sorry Cam. Can't make it tonight. Give Hank my love.

I frowned because I knew Elle had been looking forward to the party all week. I didn't ask questions though. I sent a thumbs up and threw back a shot as I stood to my feet.

With calculated steps I marched up onto the stage and motioned over the lead singer. "Y'all know any songs by the Judd's?"

He laughed. "Hell yeah."

"May I?" I asked.

He handed me the cordless microphone and I walked over to center stage. Tilly and Bekka whistled, while cheers broke out as the band started the familiar tune.

"Is there a Jace Foster in the house tonight?" I asked into the mic.

Everyone clapped and Jace smiled from his position at the bar, lifting his beer to me in recognition.

I winked. "This one's for you, detective."

The end.

Thank You

Thank you for reading Whispers of Timber Creek! I hope you enjoyed these characters as much as I enjoyed writing them!

Curious about Elle and Easton's story?
Confessions of Timber Creek is a second chance, single dad, nanny romance filled with small town secrets.

Coming SEP 29th!

For information on future release dates be sure to sign up for my newsletter or follow me on social media

http://www.authorsjchaynie.com

ACKNOWLEDGMENTS

First off, I want to thank my readers! You are what keep me going and keep me up until ungodly hours of the night just so I can bring these stories to life for you! Thank you! I want to thank my husband, even though he has never read a single book I have written, nor does he plan to, has always been a trooper when I go on and on about a new book idea, or spend hours on the computer perfecting every aspect of a new story. My family and friends who support me in every way, and for my die hard book besties who literally talk through the entire plot with me before it's even on paper. I love you all. It takes a village and I'm so thankful for mine! I loved creating a new and exciting town. Honestly, this book was a tricky one, and I restarted about three times, but once the words started flowing, I fell in love with Jace and Camille, along with the rest of the crew. Thank you all for your love and support. It is never forgotten.

About Author

S.J. Chaynie is a small-town Texas girl who has found a love for writing. She enjoys writing romance, with a sprinkle of suspense, and a little humor. If she is not busy writing her newest ideas, she is spending time with her husband and two beautiful daughters. She believes a good book and a lot of laughs is the best medicine. She brings suspense, love, angst, and sometimes the occasional heartbreak to her stories. Always a HEA, but every character and story she holds close to her heart and hopes they touch yours as well.